EOD SOLDIERS

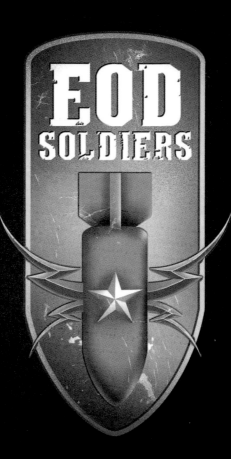

EOD Soldiers is published by Stone Arch Books,
A Capstone Imprint
1710 Roe Crest Drive
North Mankato, Minnesota 56003
www.mycapstone.com

Text and illustrations © 2017

Library of Congress Cataloging-in-Publication Data is available on the
Library of Congress website.

ISBN: 978-1-4965-3108-7 (library binding)
ISBN: 978-1-4965-3112-4 (eBook PDF)

Summary: Explosive Ordnance Disposal Specialist Dan West isn't easily
rattled. He regularly risks his life to disarm IEDs and puts up with his squad
mates' mean-spirited pranks without complaint. But when West finds an
Afghan boy standing on a bomb's pressure plate, he must force himself to
remain calm. If he doesn't, West will face the only thing he truly fears: the
pink mist. The aftermath of a bomb taking someone's life.

Designer: Brann Garvey

Printed and bound in the USA.
009620F16

THE MIST

written by Matthew K. Manning
art by Rico Lima and Thiago Dal Bello

STONE ARCH BOOKS
a capstone imprint

EOD
SOLDIERS

SPECIALIST DAN WEST:

West is pretty serious about his job. He knows what he's doing and doesn't lack for confidence.

PRIVATE TOMMY BADGER:

Badger is a quintessential all-American, but with a chip on his shoulder the size of a conjoined twin.

SPECIALIST ROSE CAMPBELL:

Campbell is a no-nonsense soldier who is extremely proud of her position in the military.

LIEUTENANT (LT) BRANCH:

As the commanding officer of their road clearing crew, Branch is a tough leader with an even tougher demeanor.

MOUSER:

West's best friend and a loyal labrador retriever, Mouser is trained to sniff out IEDs.

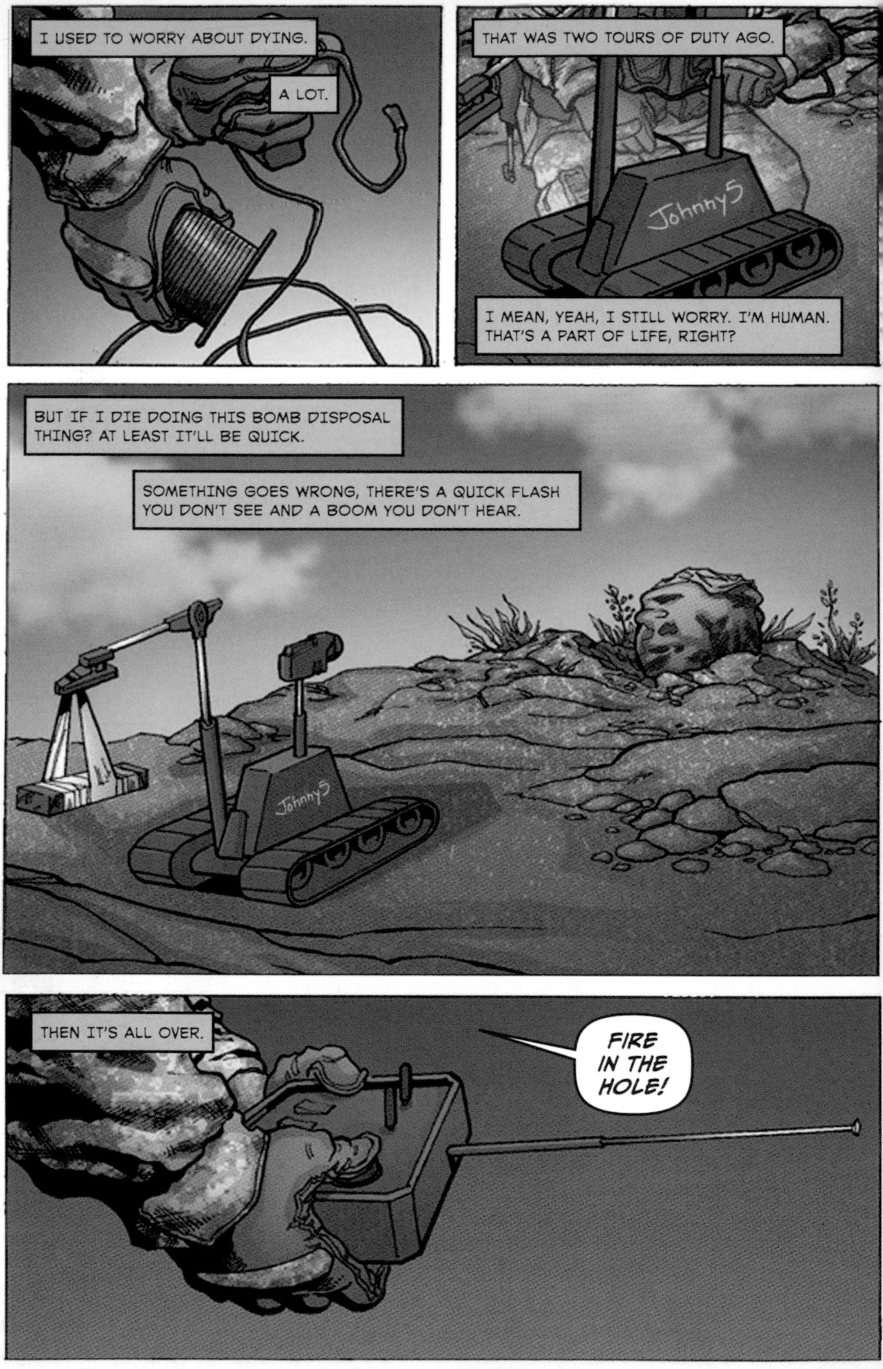
I USED TO WORRY ABOUT DYING.
A LOT.
THAT WAS TWO TOURS OF DUTY AGO.
Johnny5
I MEAN, YEAH, I STILL WORRY. I'M HUMAN. THAT'S A PART OF LIFE, RIGHT?
BUT IF I DIE DOING THIS BOMB DISPOSAL THING? AT LEAST IT'LL BE QUICK.
SOMETHING GOES WRONG, THERE'S A QUICK FLASH YOU DON'T SEE AND A BOOM YOU DON'T HEAR.
Johnny5
THEN IT'S ALL OVER.
FIRE IN THE HOLE!

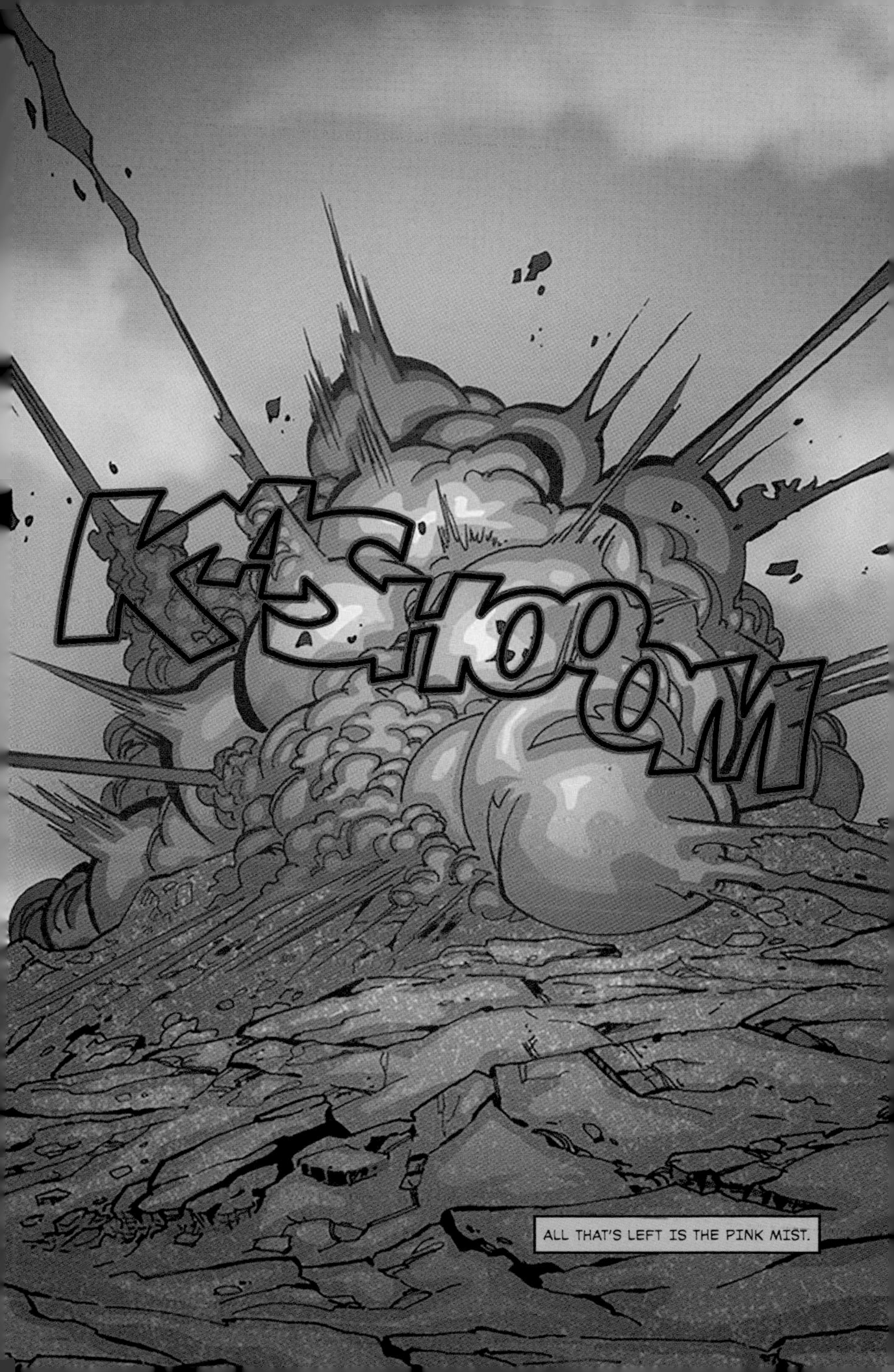
KA-SHOOOOM
ALL THAT'S LEFT IS THE PINK MIST.

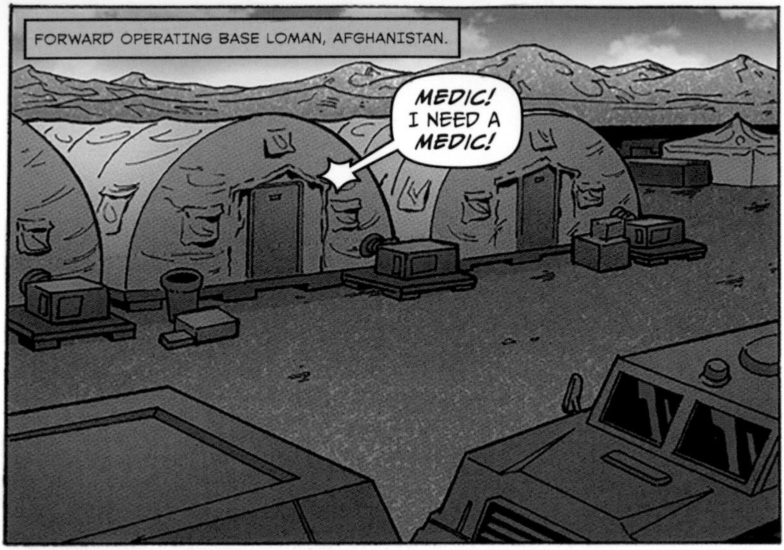
FORWARD OPERATING BASE LOMAN, AFGHANISTAN.
MEDIC! I NEED A MEDIC!

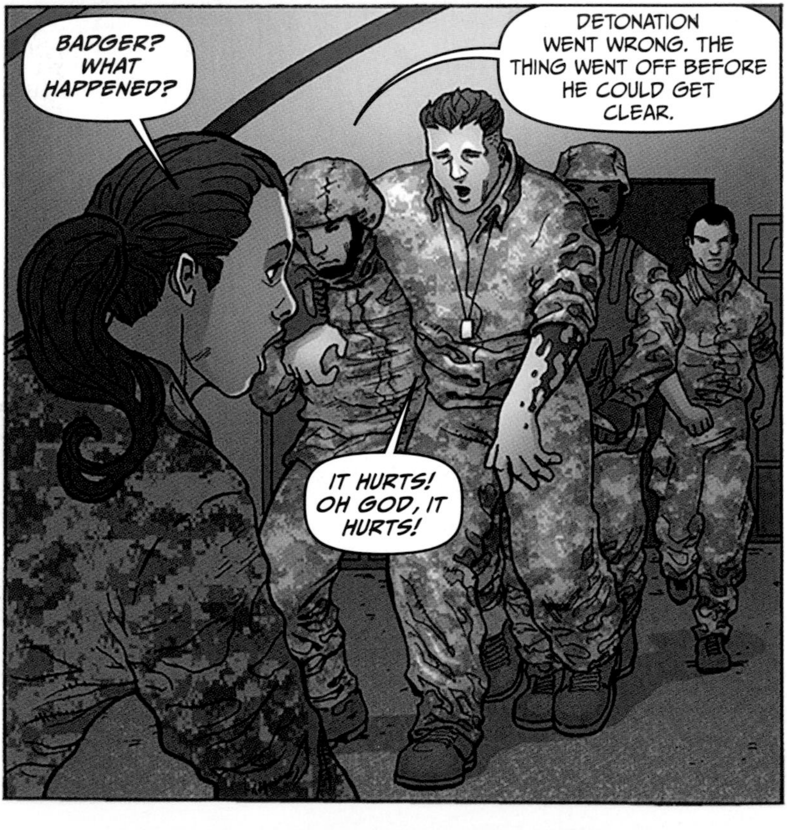
BADGER? WHAT HAPPENED?
DETONATION WENT WRONG. THE THING WENT OFF BEFORE HE COULD GET CLEAR.
IT HURTS! OH GOD, IT HURTS!

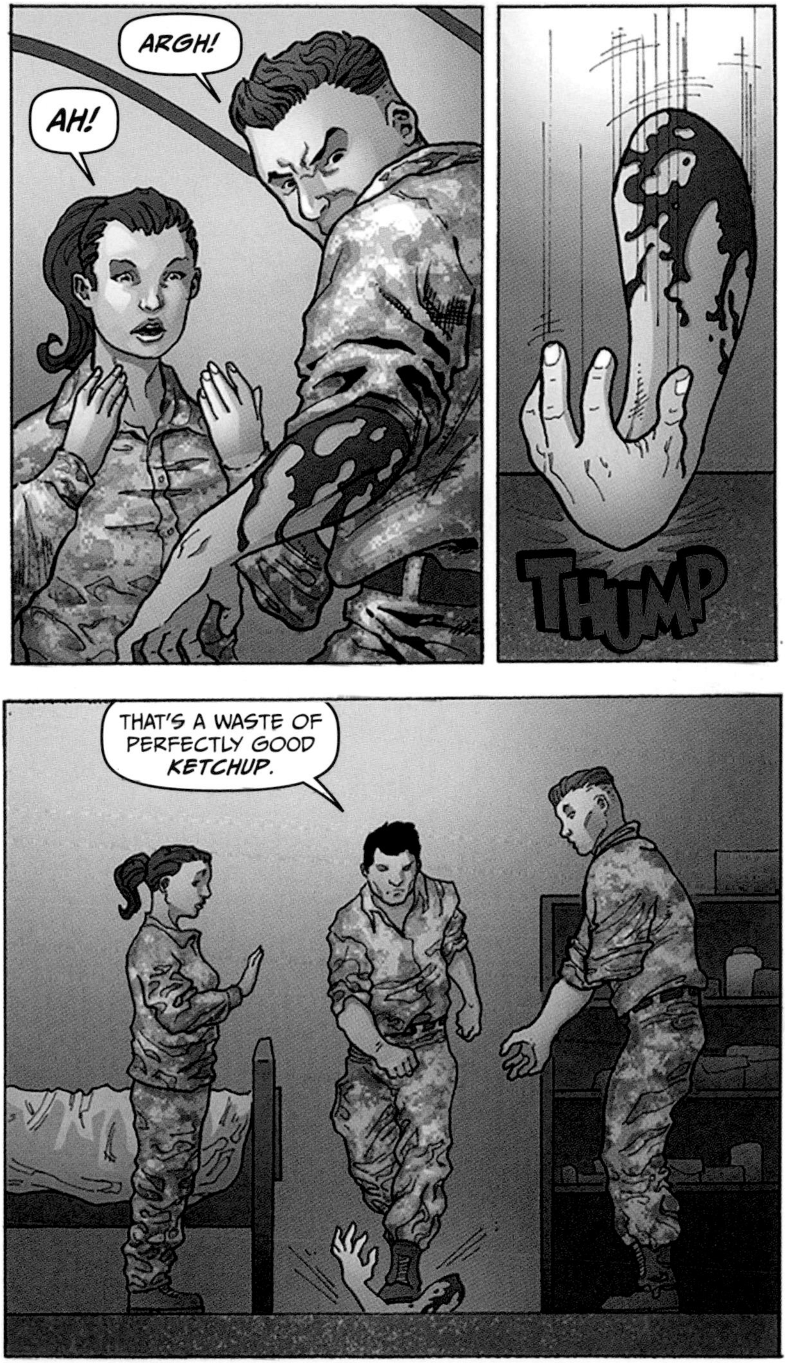
ARGH!
AH!
THUMP
THAT'S A WASTE OF PERFECTLY GOOD KETCHUP.

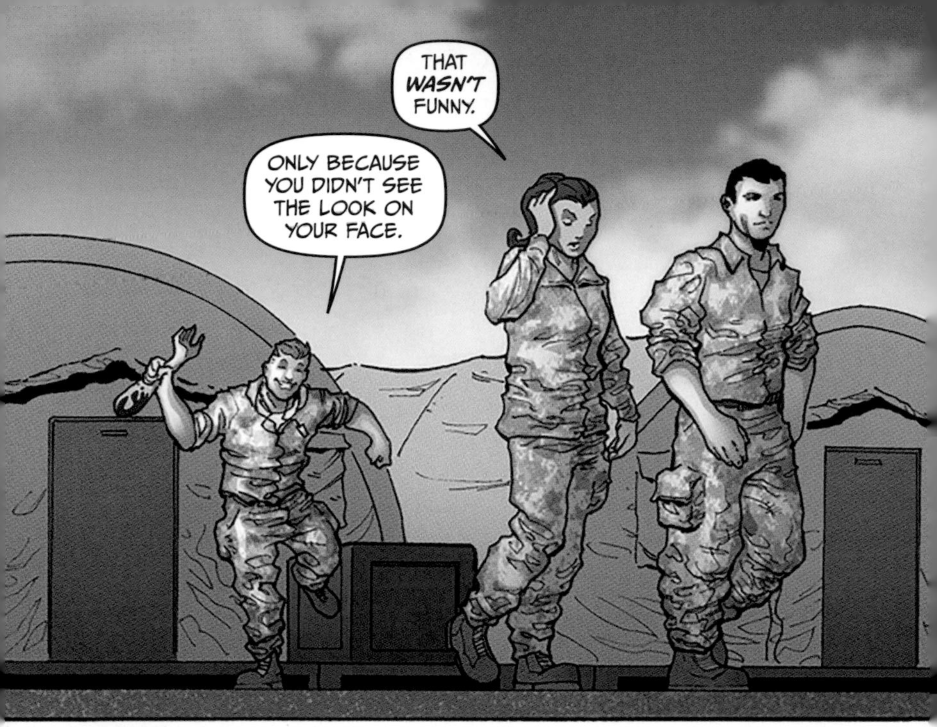
THAT WASN'T FUNNY.
ONLY BECAUSE YOU DIDN'T SEE THE LOOK ON YOUR FACE.

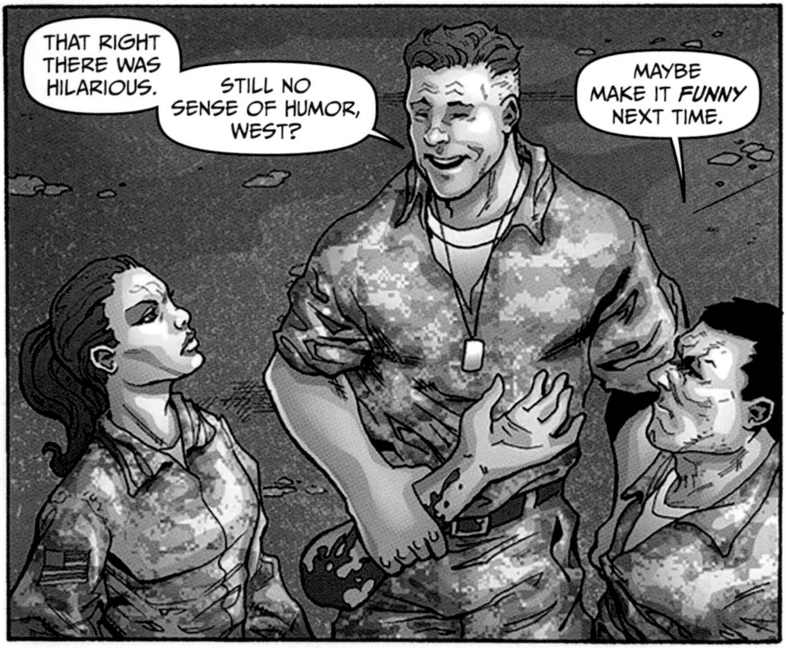
THAT RIGHT THERE WAS HILARIOUS.
STILL NO SENSE OF HUMOR, WEST?
MAYBE MAKE IT FUNNY NEXT TIME.

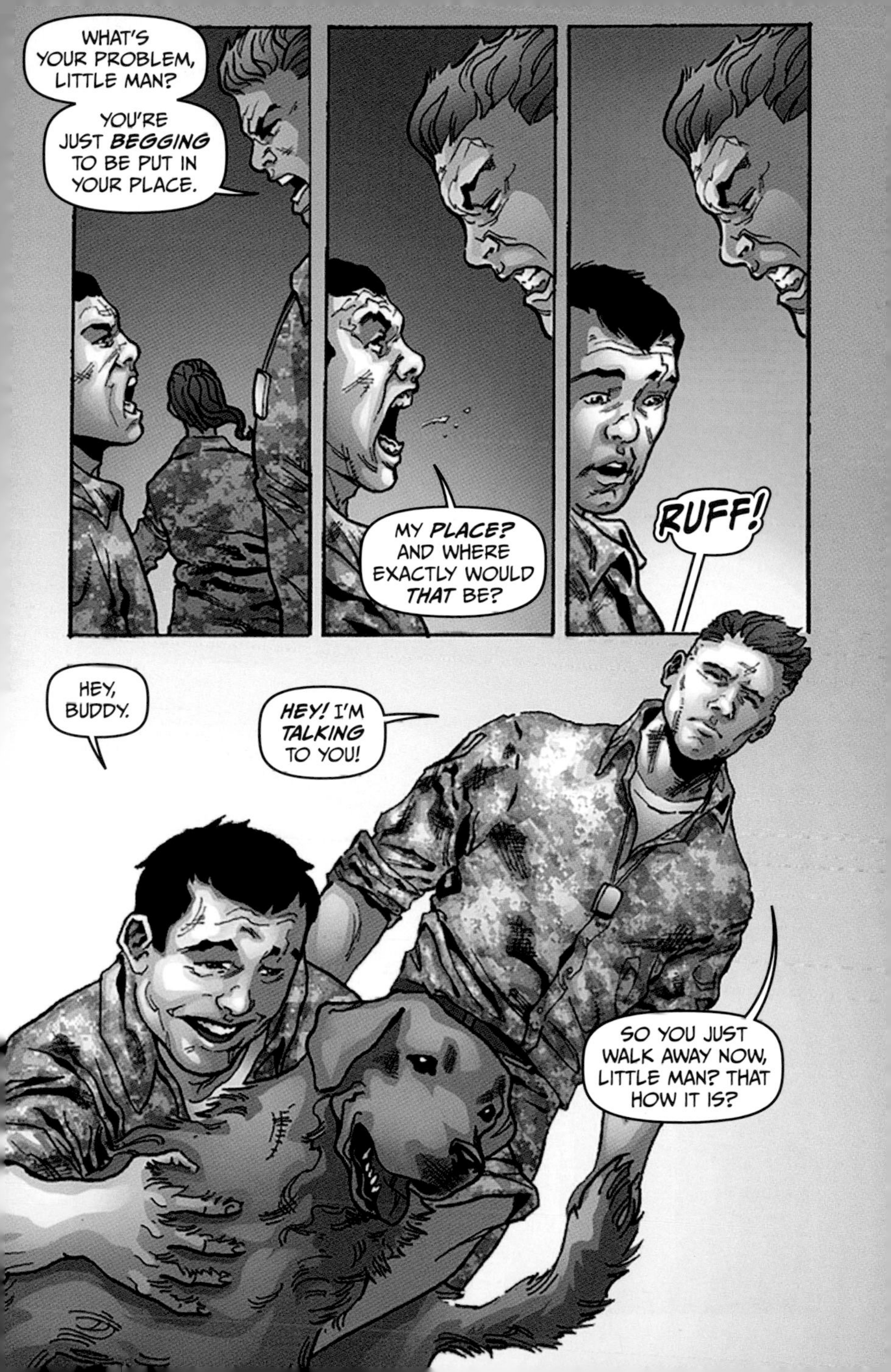
WHAT'S YOUR PROBLEM, LITTLE MAN?
YOU'RE JUST BEGGING TO BE PUT IN YOUR PLACE.
MY PLACE? AND WHERE EXACTLY WOULD THAT BE?
RUFF!
HEY, BUDDY.
HEY! I'M TALKING TO YOU!
SO YOU JUST WALK AWAY NOW, LITTLE MAN? THAT HOW IT IS?

MOUSER'S BEEN AT FOB LOMAN ALMOST AS LONG AS I HAVE.

I OWE HIM A LOT.

MY FIRST NIGHT HERE, I SAW A MOUSE IN MY BED. SAW ANOTHER ONE THE SECOND NIGHT.

THIRD NIGHT, I CAUGHT ONE.

FOR YOUR SAKE, I HOPE YOU NEVER HAVE TO KILL A MOUSE WITH YOUR BARE HANDS.

THEY BROUGHT IN MOUSER A FEW WEEKS LATER TO SNIFF OUT IEDS*. AS IT TURNS OUT, HE'S ALSO ONE HECK OF A HUNTER.

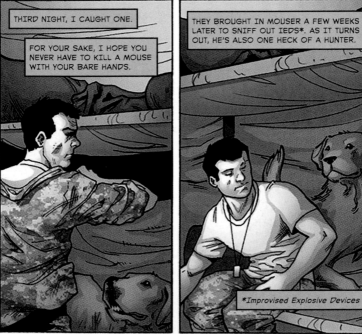

*Improvised Explosive Devices

OUR ENTIRE CAMP WAS MOUSE-FREE IN TWO DAYS.

GOOD BOY, MOUSER.

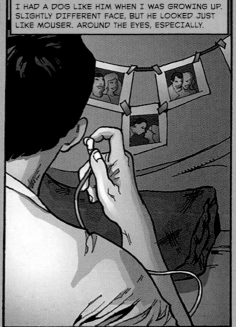

I HAD A DOG LIKE HIM WHEN I WAS GROWING UP. SLIGHTLY DIFFERENT FACE, BUT HE LOOKED JUST LIKE MOUSER. AROUND THE EYES, ESPECIALLY.

I MISS THAT DOG.

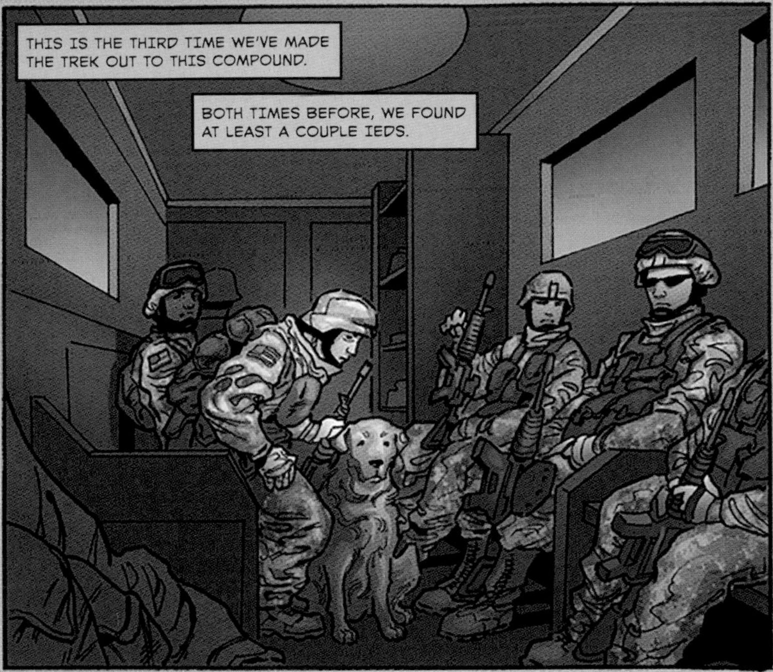
THIS IS THE THIRD TIME WE'VE MADE THE TREK OUT TO THIS COMPOUND.
BOTH TIMES BEFORE, WE FOUND AT LEAST A COUPLE IEDS.

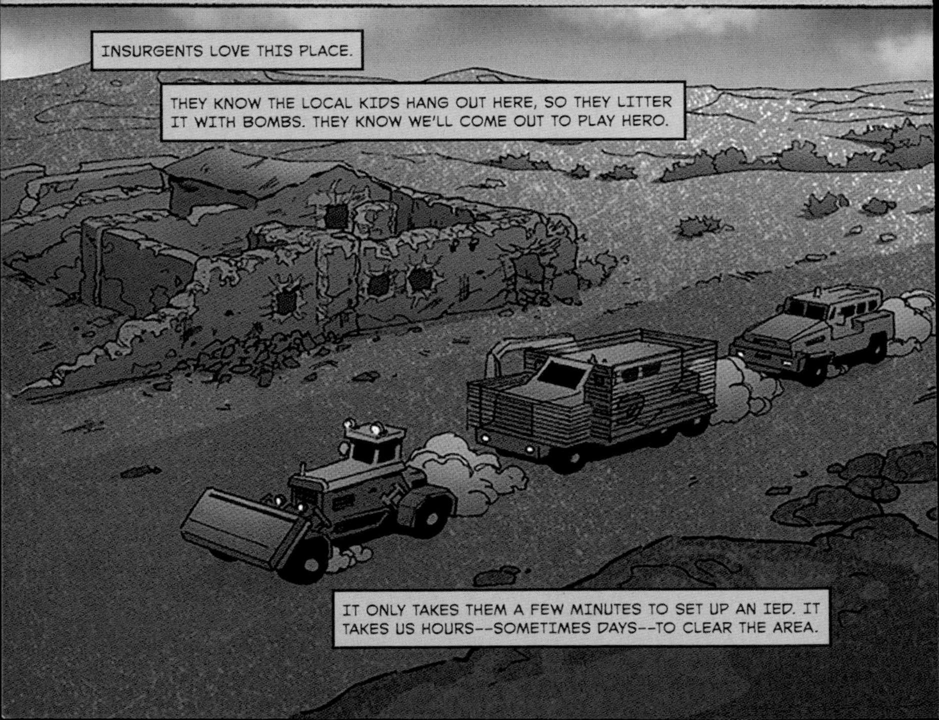
INSURGENTS LOVE THIS PLACE.
THEY KNOW THE LOCAL KIDS HANG OUT HERE, SO THEY LITTER IT WITH BOMBS. THEY KNOW WE'LL COME OUT TO PLAY HERO.
IT ONLY TAKES THEM A FEW MINUTES TO SET UP AN IED. IT TAKES US HOURS--SOMETIMES DAYS--TO CLEAR THE AREA.

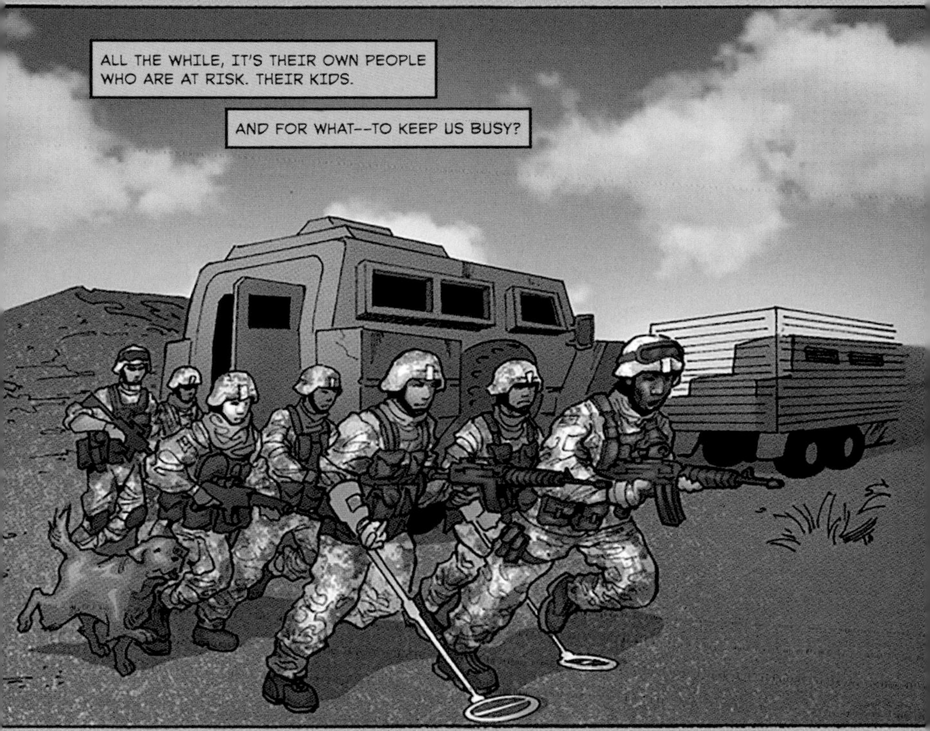
ALL THE WHILE, IT'S THEIR OWN PEOPLE WHO ARE AT RISK. THEIR KIDS.
AND FOR WHAT--TO KEEP US BUSY?

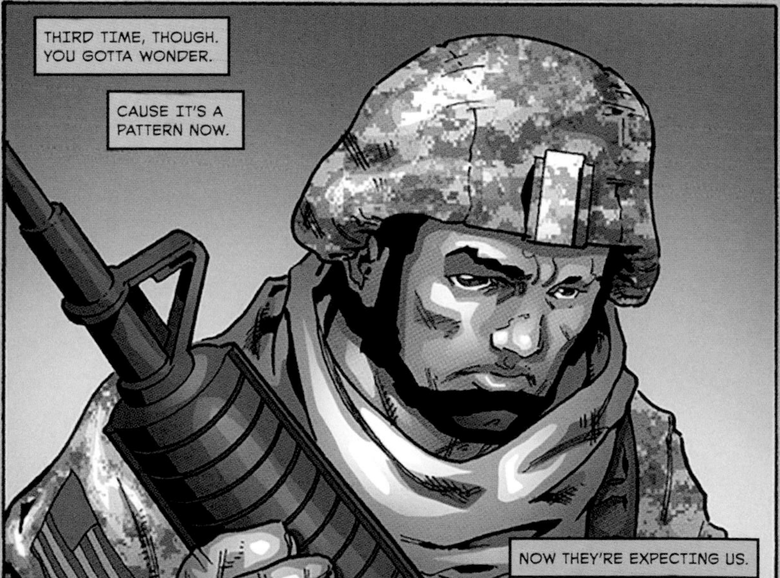
THIRD TIME, THOUGH. YOU GOTTA WONDER.
CAUSE IT'S A PATTERN NOW.
NOW THEY'RE EXPECTING US.

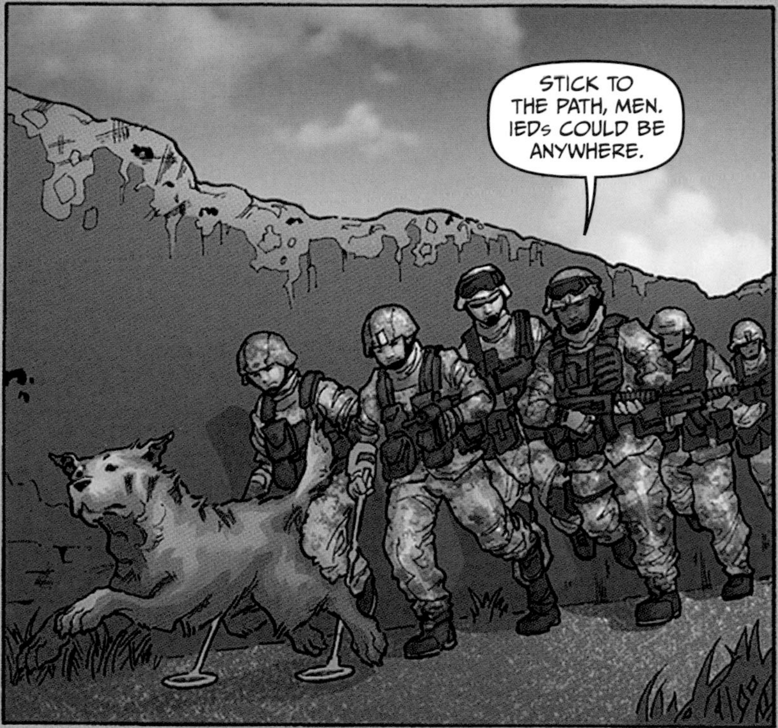
STICK TO THE PATH, MEN. IEDs COULD BE ANYWHERE.

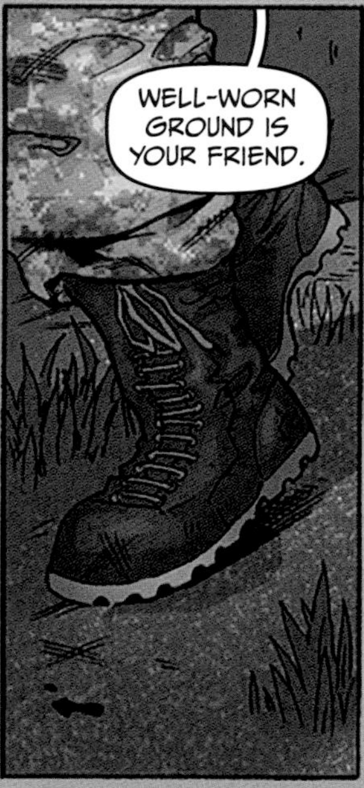
WELL-WORN GROUND IS YOUR FRIEND.

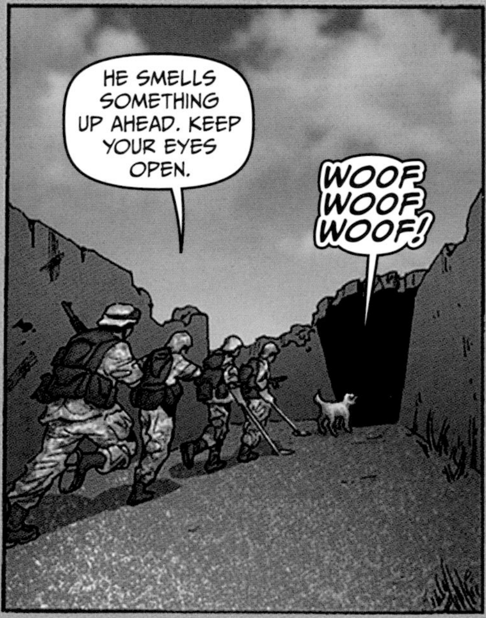
HE SMELLS SOMETHING UP AHEAD. KEEP YOUR EYES OPEN.
WOOF WOOF WOOF!

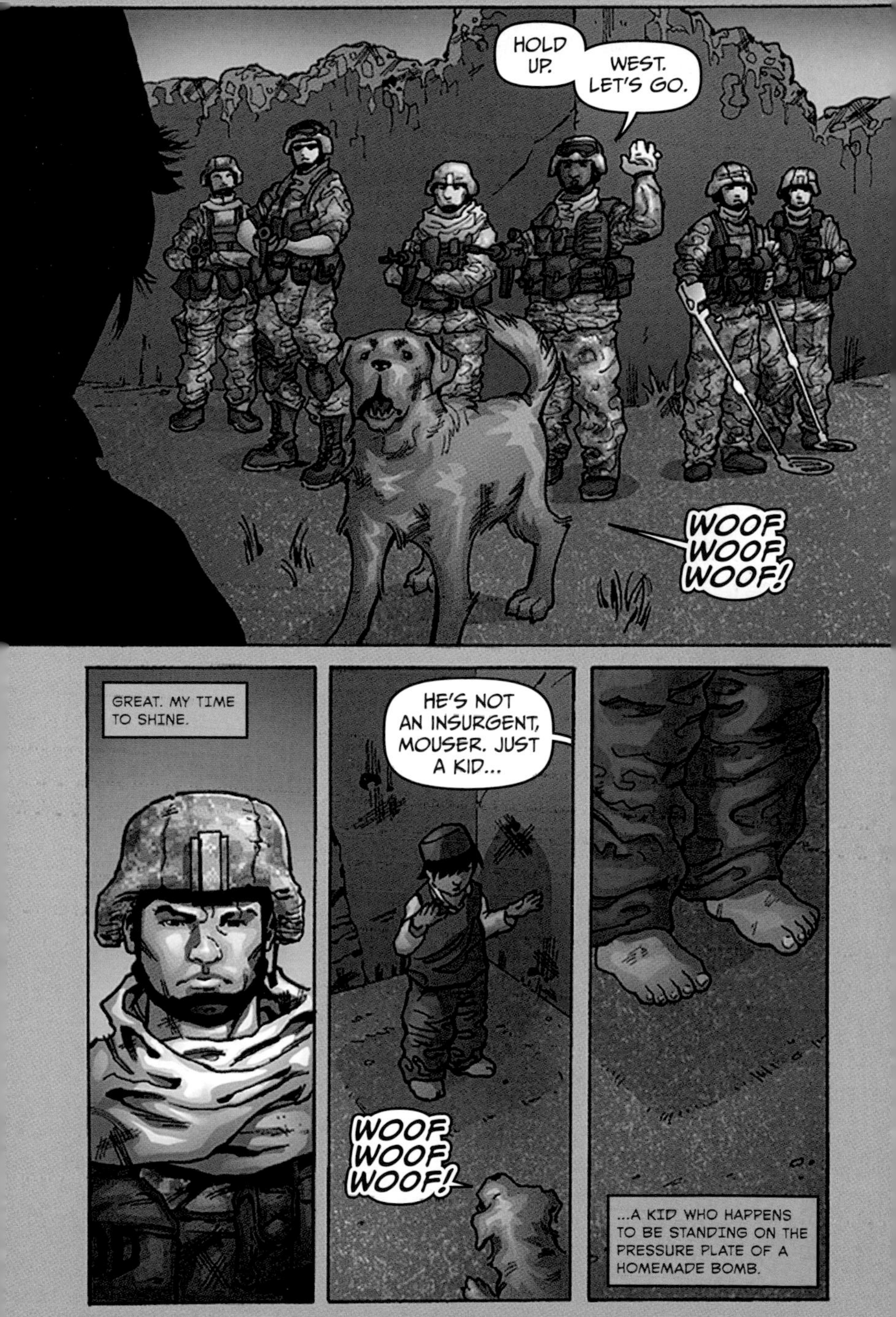
HOLD UP.
WEST. LET'S GO.
WOOF WOOF WOOF!
GREAT. MY TIME TO SHINE.
HE'S NOT AN INSURGENT, MOUSER. JUST A KID...
WOOF WOOF WOOF!
...A KID WHO HAPPENS TO BE STANDING ON THE PRESSURE PLATE OF A HOMEMADE BOMB.

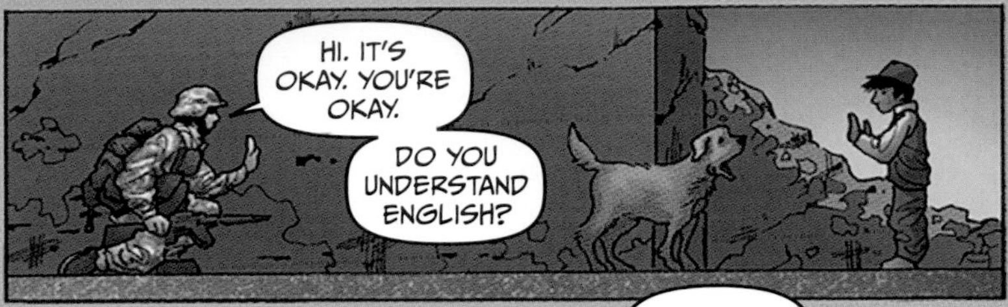
HI. IT'S OKAY. YOU'RE OKAY.
DO YOU UNDERSTAND ENGLISH?

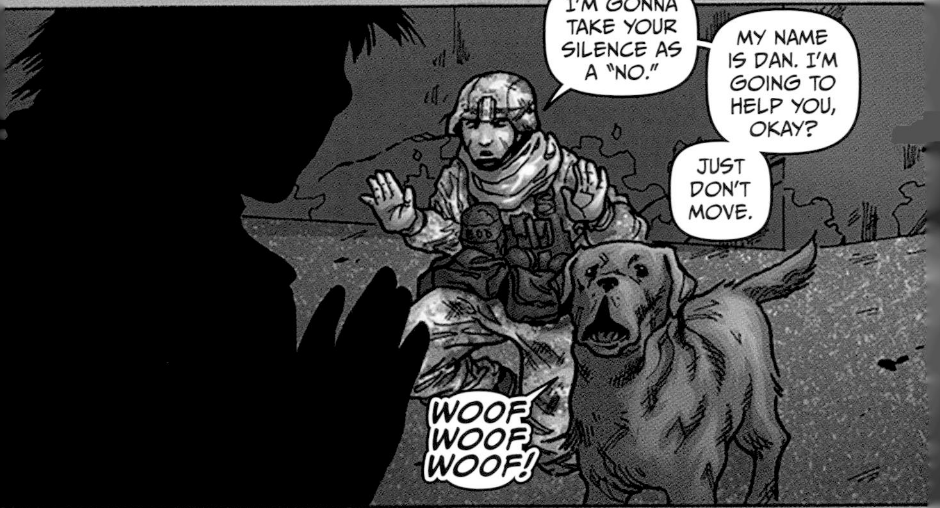
I'M GONNA TAKE YOUR SILENCE AS A "NO."
MY NAME IS DAN. I'M GOING TO HELP YOU, OKAY?
JUST DON'T MOVE.
WOOF WOOF WOOF!

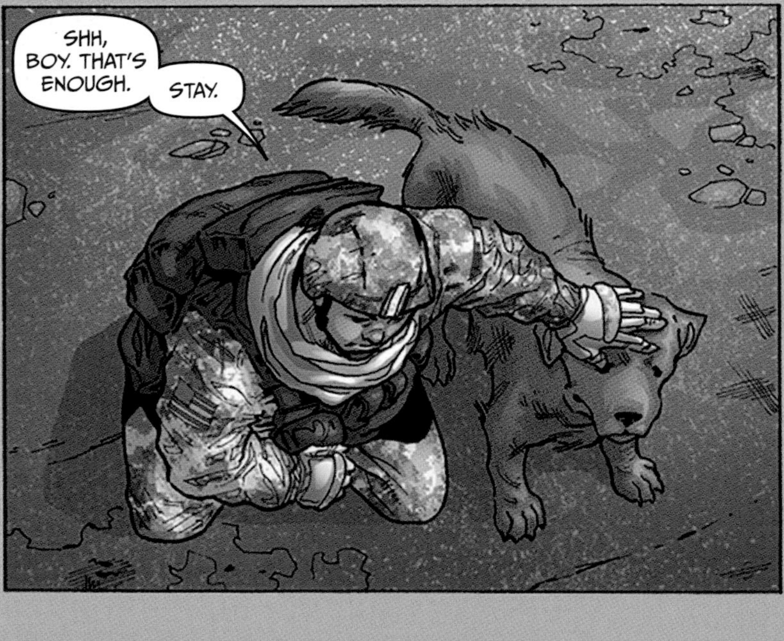
SHH, BOY. THAT'S ENOUGH.
STAY.

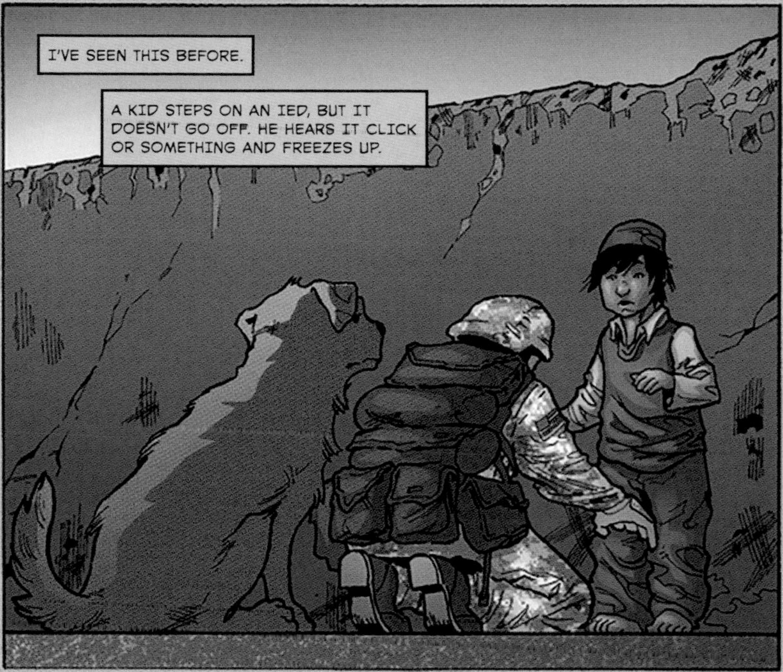
I'VE SEEN THIS BEFORE.
A KID STEPS ON AN IED, BUT IT DOESN'T GO OFF. HE HEARS IT CLICK OR SOMETHING AND FREEZES UP.

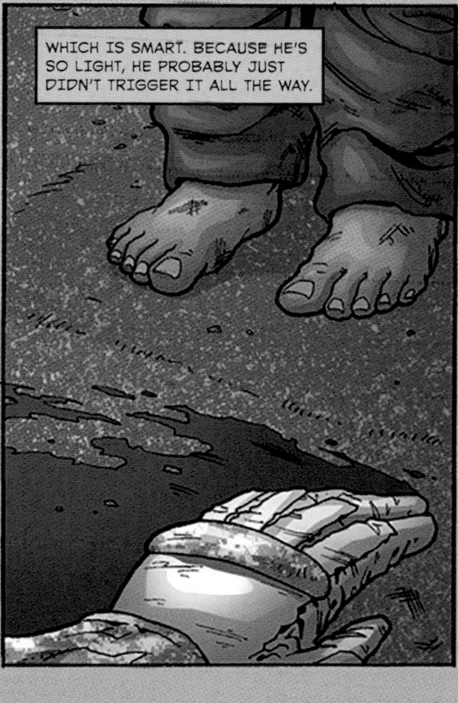
WHICH IS SMART. BECAUSE HE'S SO LIGHT, HE PROBABLY JUST DIDN'T TRIGGER IT ALL THE WAY.

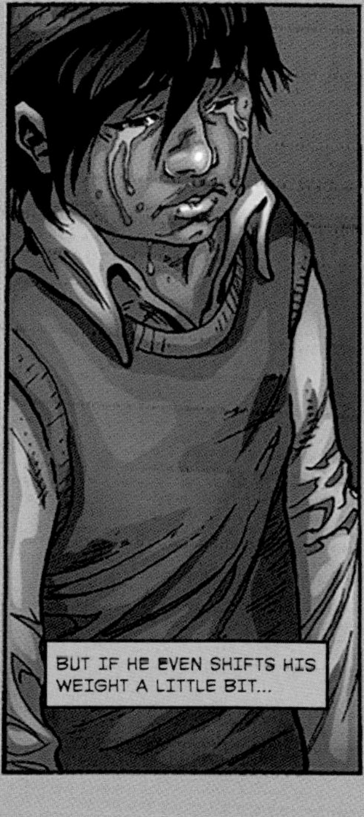
BUT IF HE EVEN SHIFTS HIS WEIGHT A LITTLE BIT...

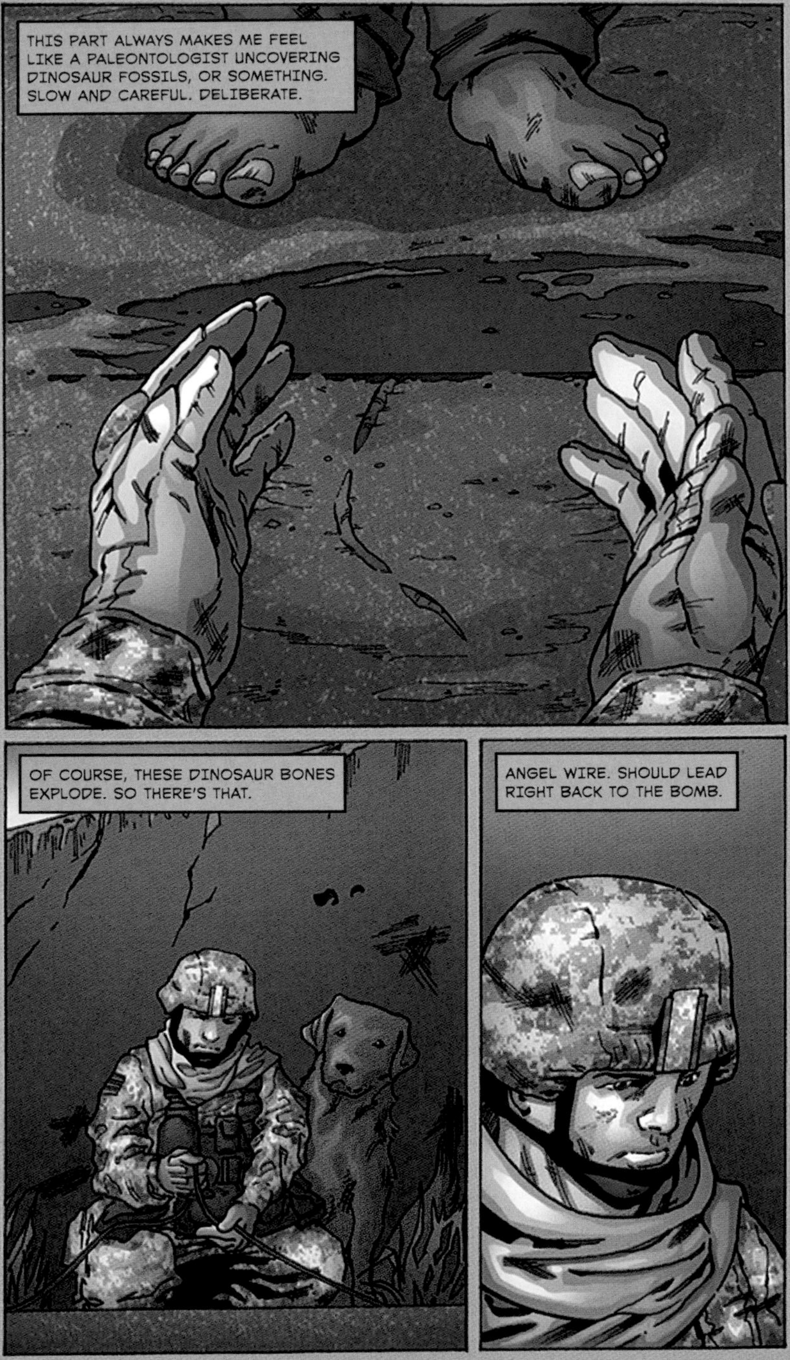
THIS PART ALWAYS MAKES ME FEEL LIKE A PALEONTOLOGIST UNCOVERING DINOSAUR FOSSILS, OR SOMETHING. SLOW AND CAREFUL. DELIBERATE.
OF COURSE, THESE DINOSAUR BONES EXPLODE. SO THERE'S THAT.
ANGEL WIRE. SHOULD LEAD RIGHT BACK TO THE BOMB.

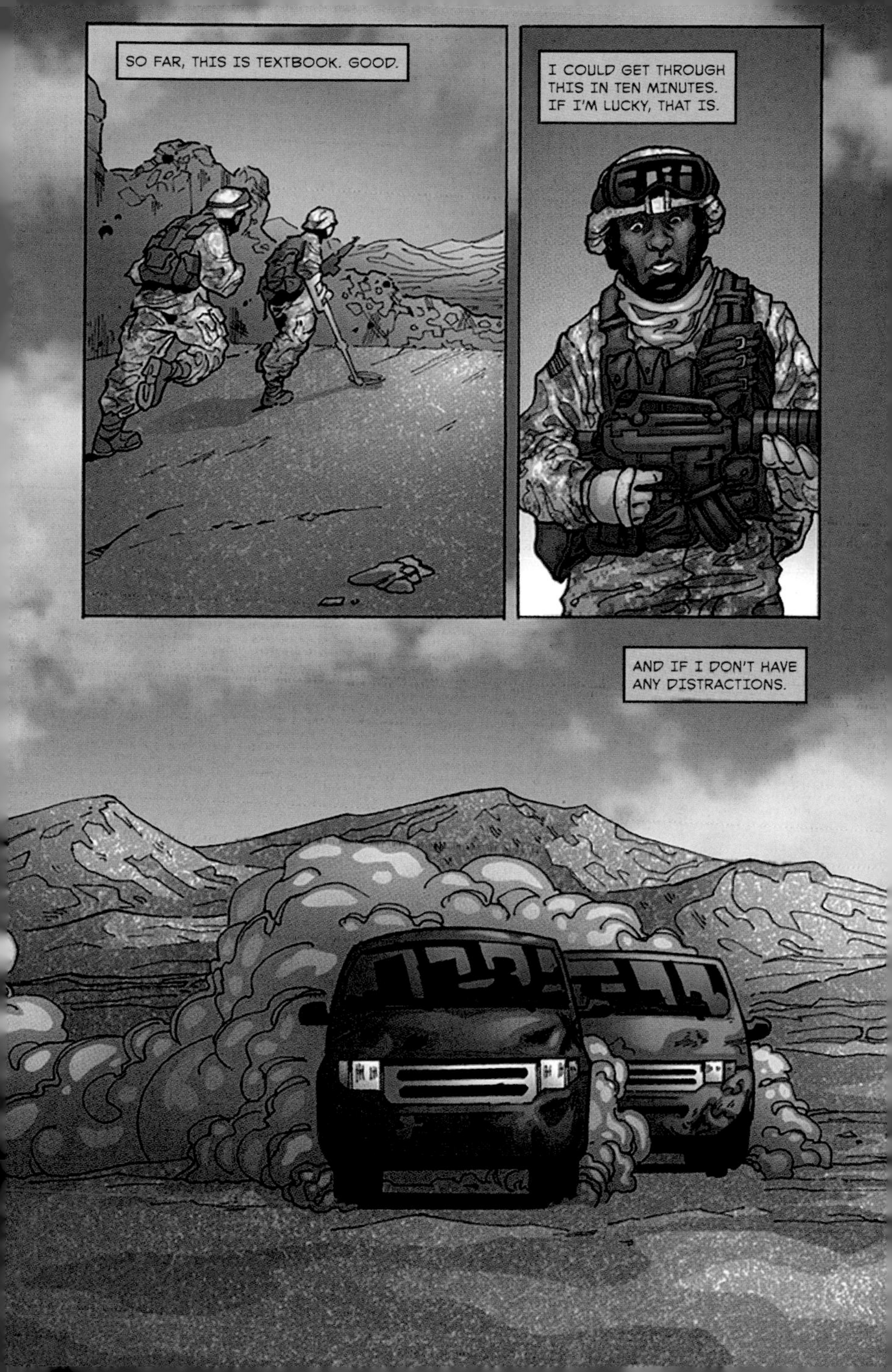
SO FAR, THIS IS TEXTBOOK. GOOD.
I COULD GET THROUGH THIS IN TEN MINUTES. IF I'M LUCKY, THAT IS.
AND IF I DON'T HAVE ANY DISTRACTIONS.

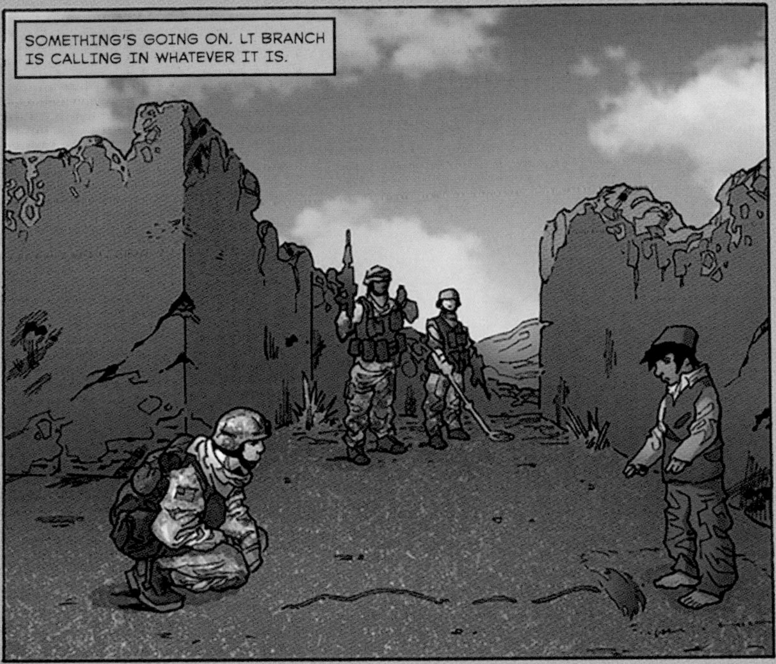
SOMETHING'S GOING ON. LT BRANCH IS CALLING IN WHATEVER IT IS.

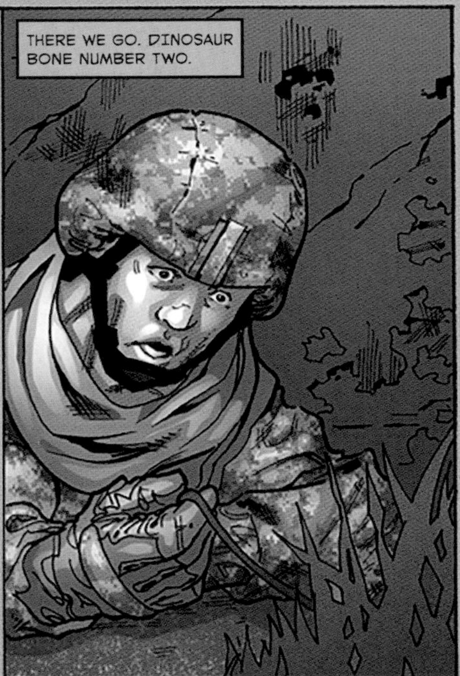
THERE WE GO. DINOSAUR BONE NUMBER TWO.

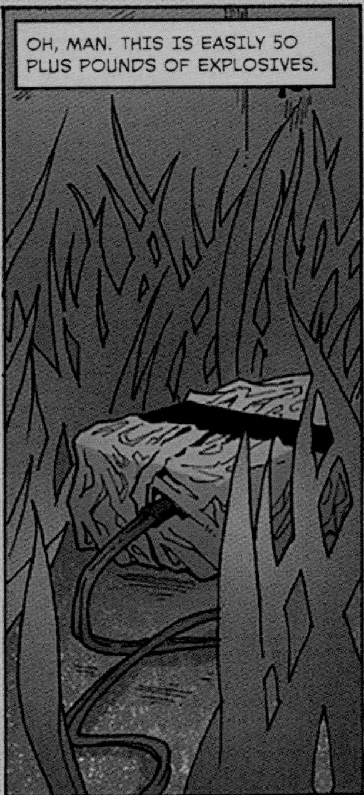
OH, MAN. THIS IS EASILY 50 PLUS POUNDS OF EXPLOSIVES.

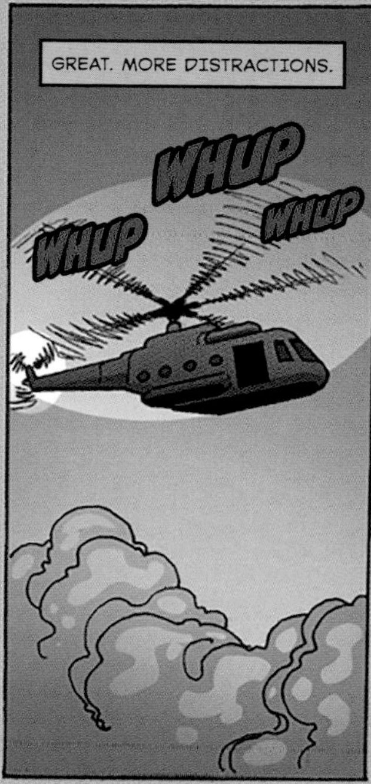
GREAT. MORE DISTRACTIONS.
WHUP
WHUP
WHUP

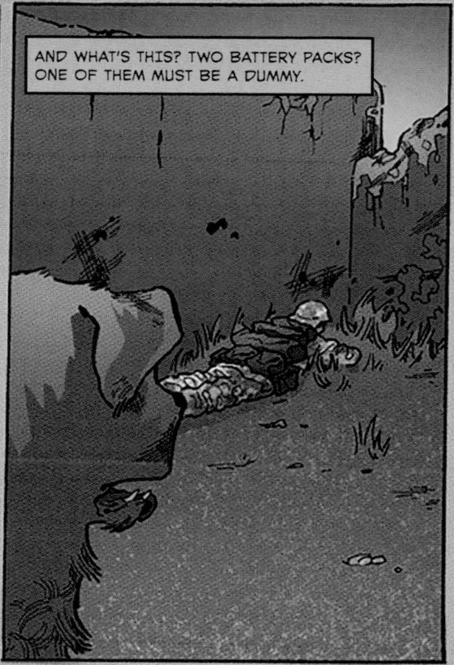
AND WHAT'S THIS? TWO BATTERY PACKS? ONE OF THEM MUST BE A DUMMY.

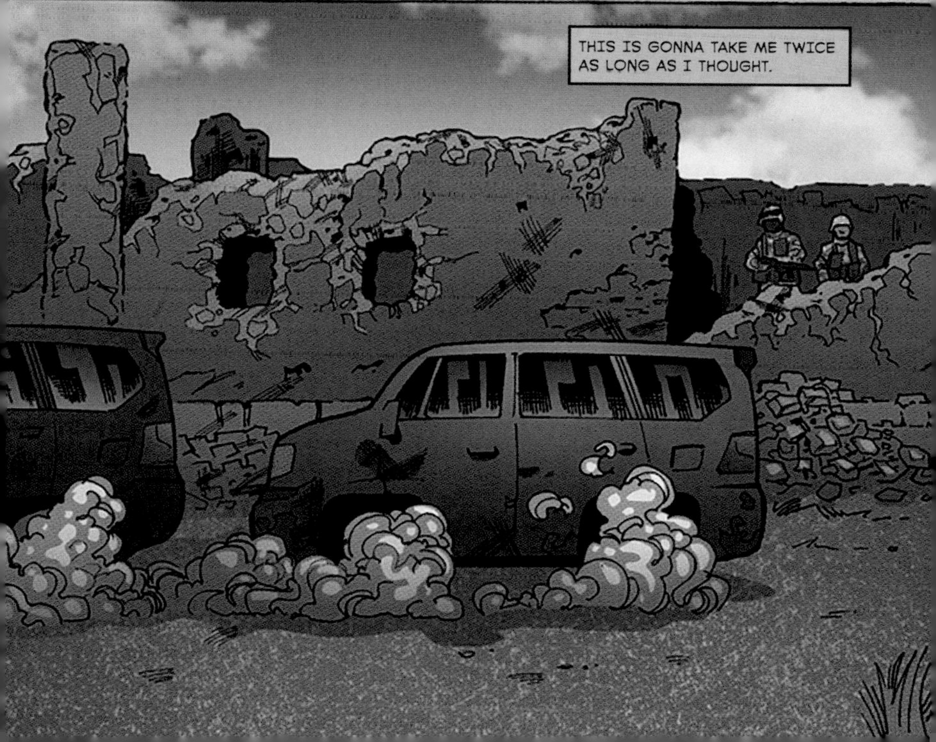
THIS IS GONNA TAKE ME TWICE AS LONG AS I THOUGHT.

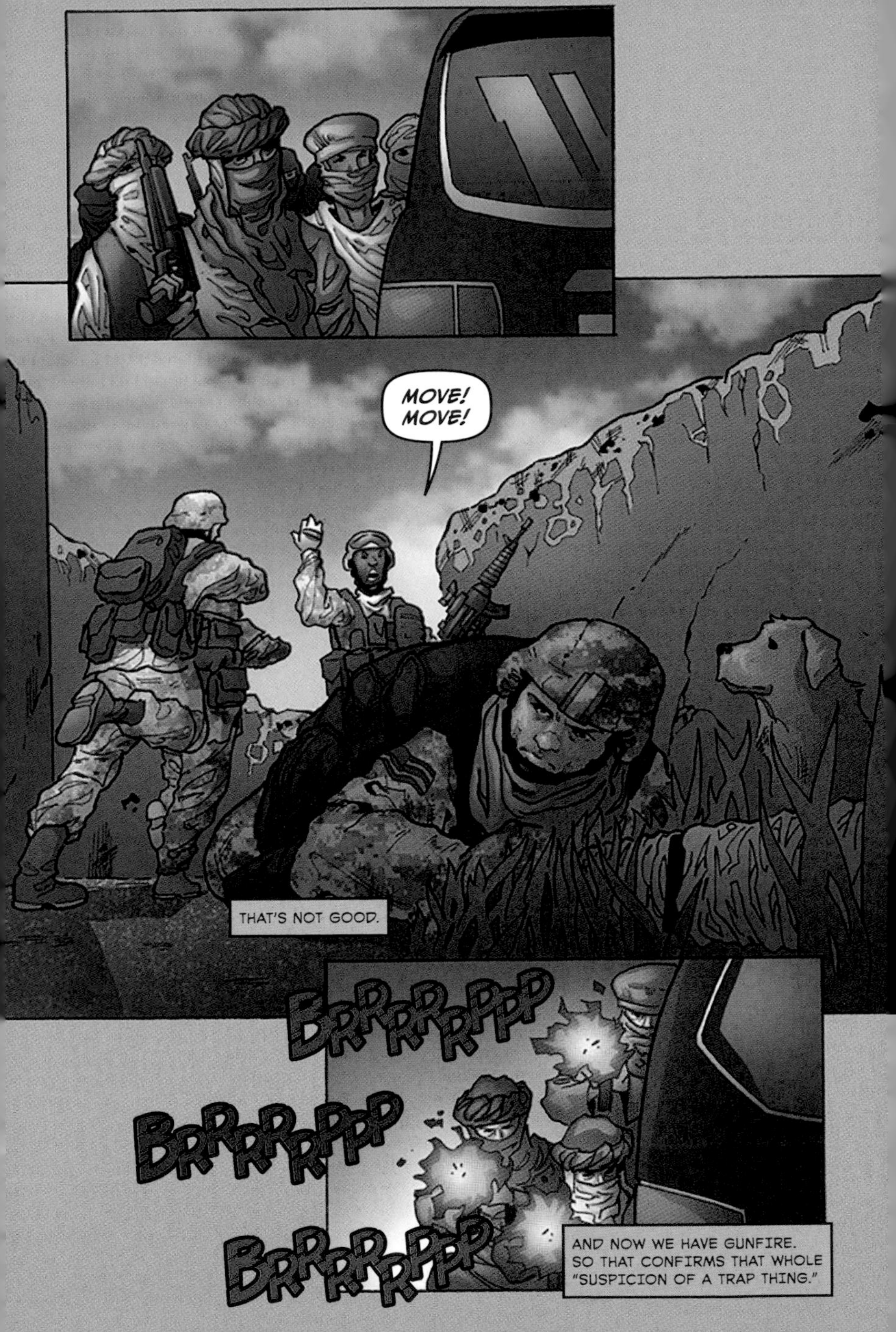
MOVE! MOVE!
THAT'S NOT GOOD.
BRRRRRRPPPP
BRRRRRRPPPP
BRRRRRRPPPP
AND NOW WE HAVE GUNFIRE. SO THAT CONFIRMS THAT WHOLE "SUSPICION OF A TRAP THING."

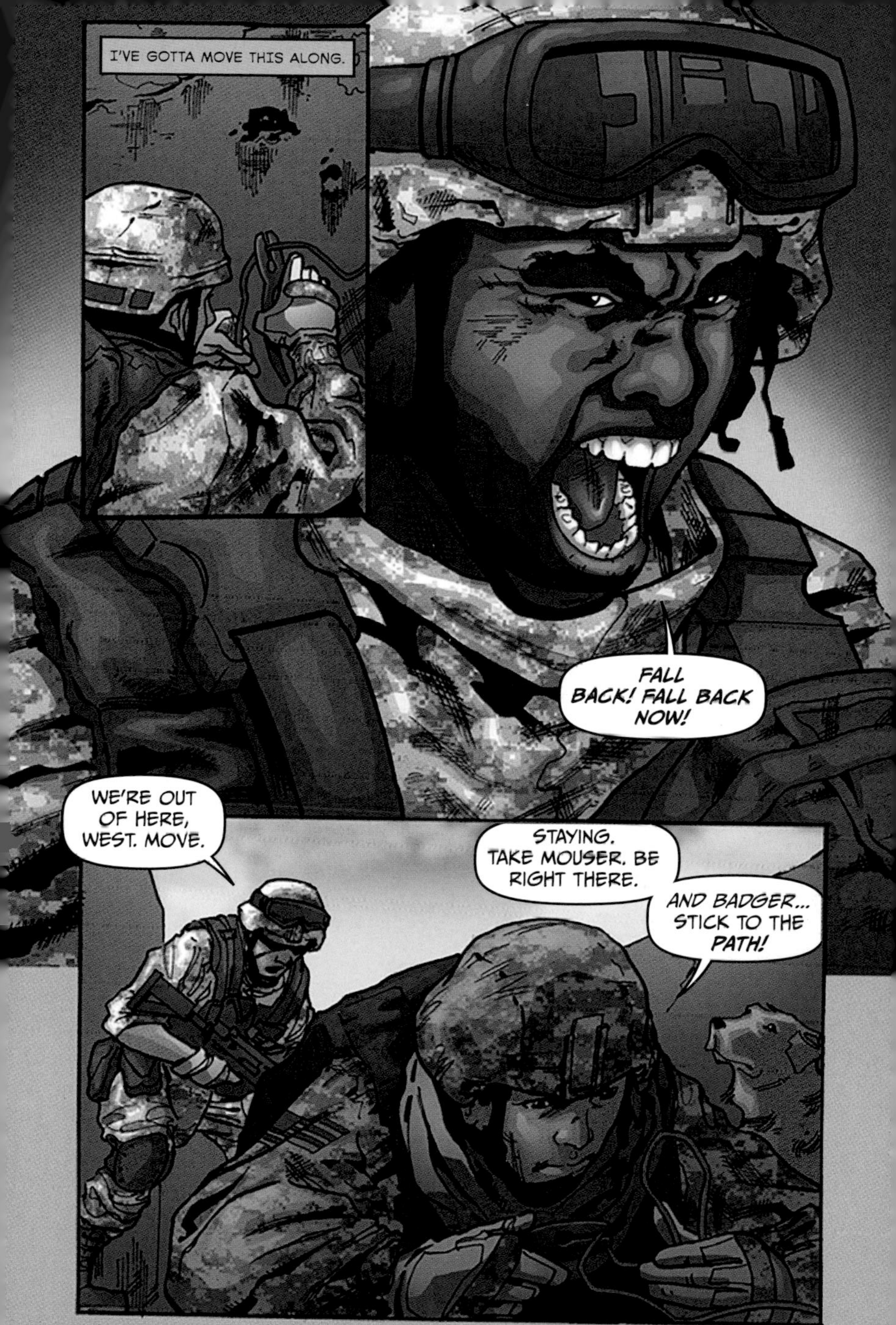
I'VE GOTTA MOVE THIS ALONG.
FALL BACK! FALL BACK NOW!
WE'RE OUT OF HERE, WEST. MOVE.
STAYING. TAKE MOUSER. BE RIGHT THERE.
AND BADGER... STICK TO THE *PATH!*

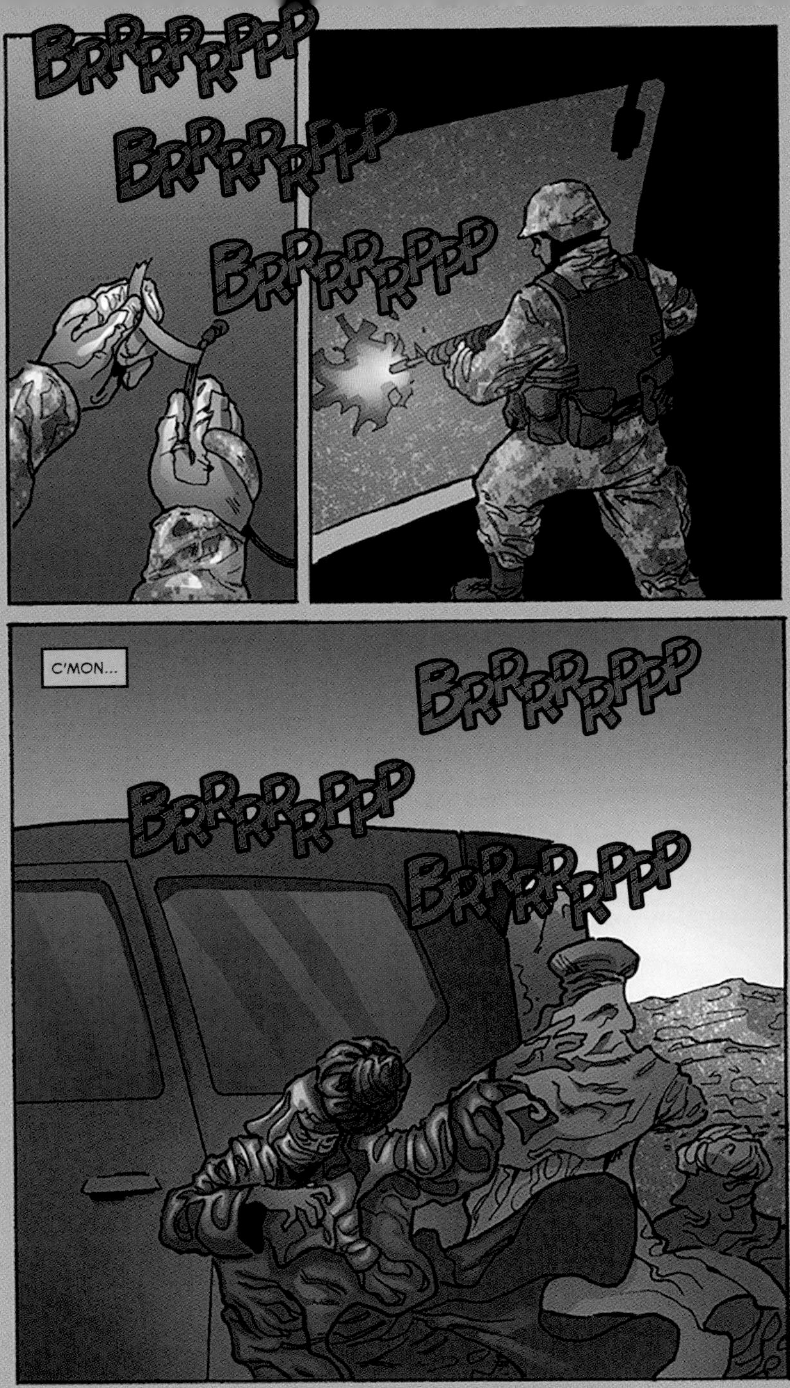
BRRRRRRPPP
BRRRRRRPPP
BRRRRRRPPP
C'MON...
BRRRRRRPPP
BRRRRRRPPP
BRRRRRRPPP

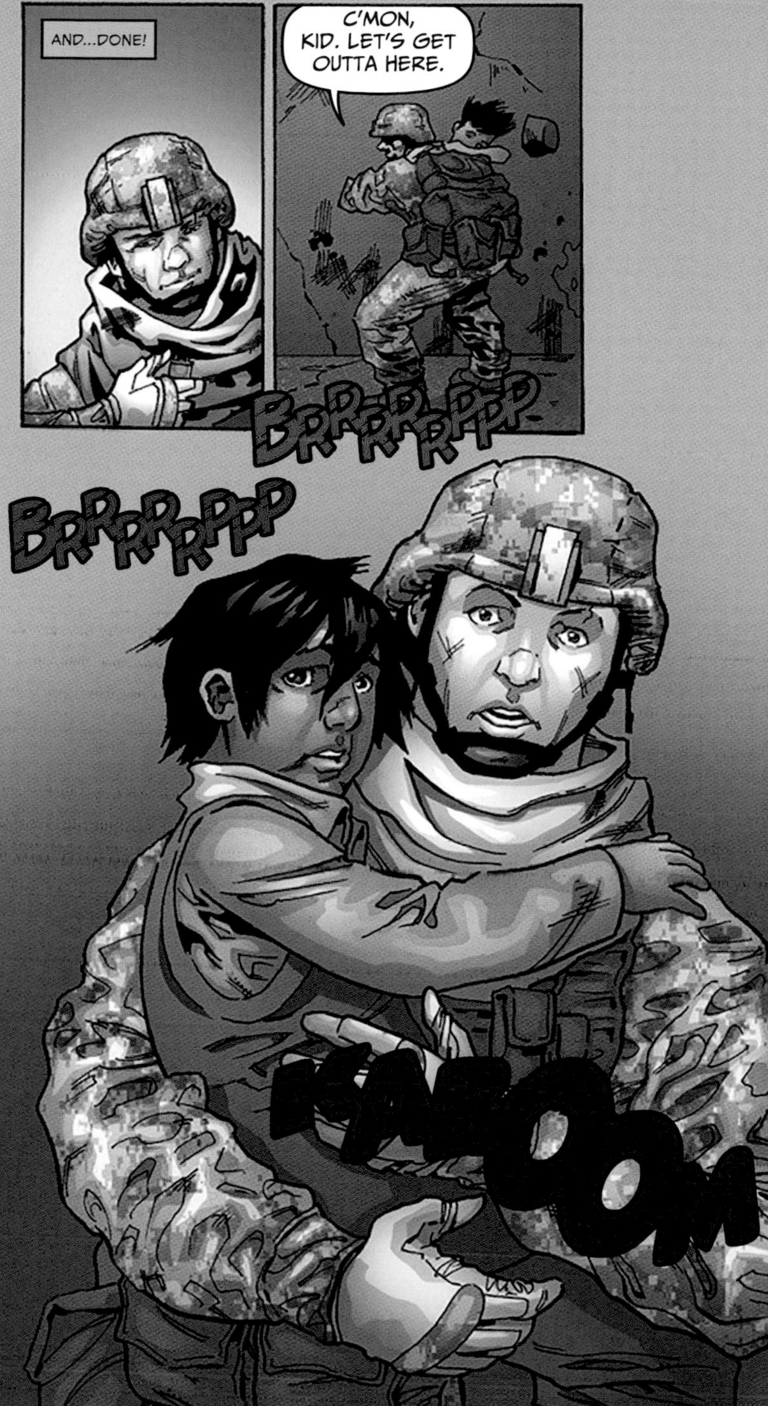
AND...DONE!
C'MON, KID. LET'S GET OUTTA HERE.
BRRRRRPPPP
BRRRRRPPPP

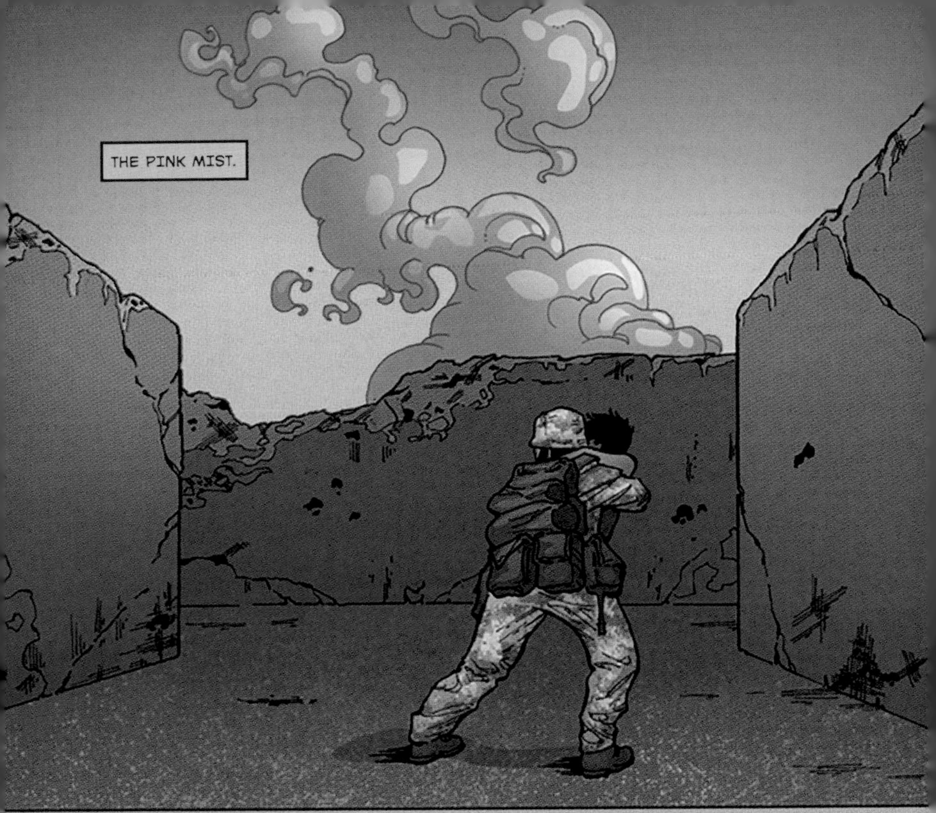
THE PINK MIST.

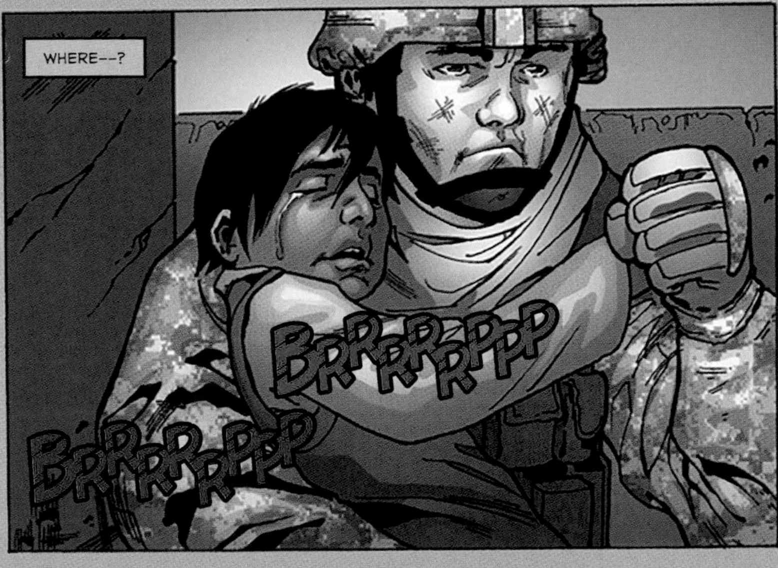
WHERE--?
BRRRRRRPPPP
BRRRRRRPPPP

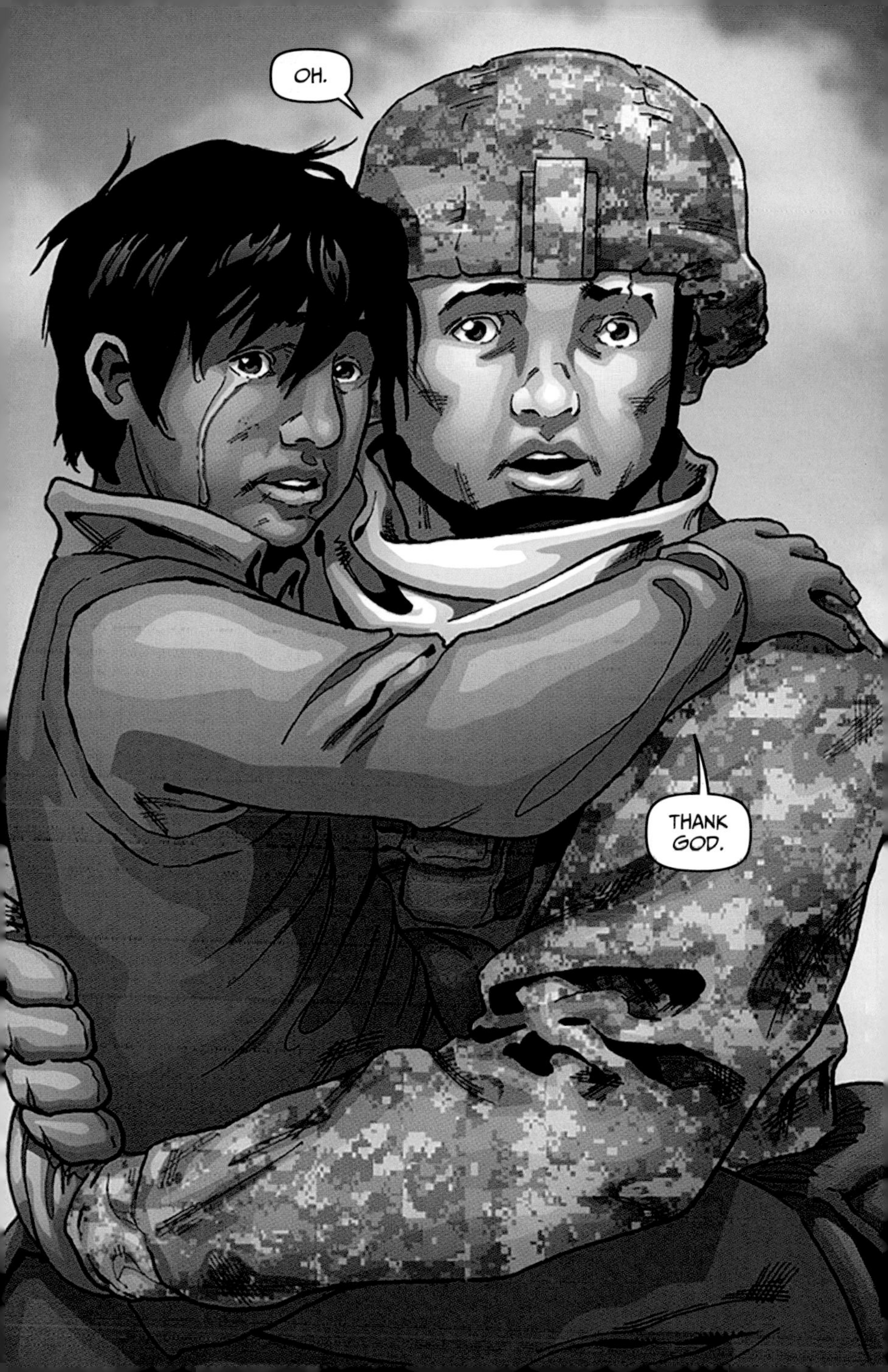
OH.
THANK GOD.

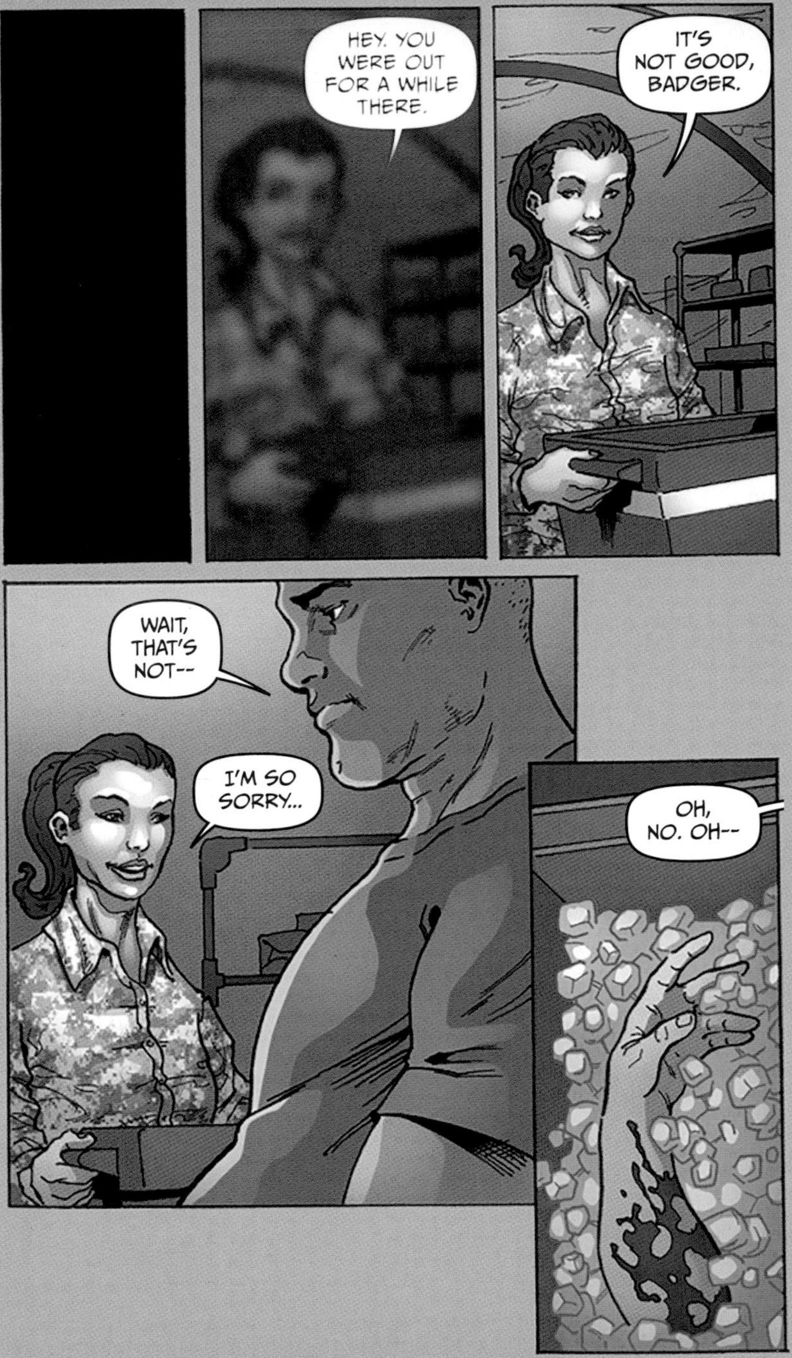
HEY. YOU WERE OUT FOR A WHILE THERE.
IT'S NOT GOOD, BADGER.
WAIT, THAT'S NOT--
I'M SO SORRY...
OH, NO. OH--

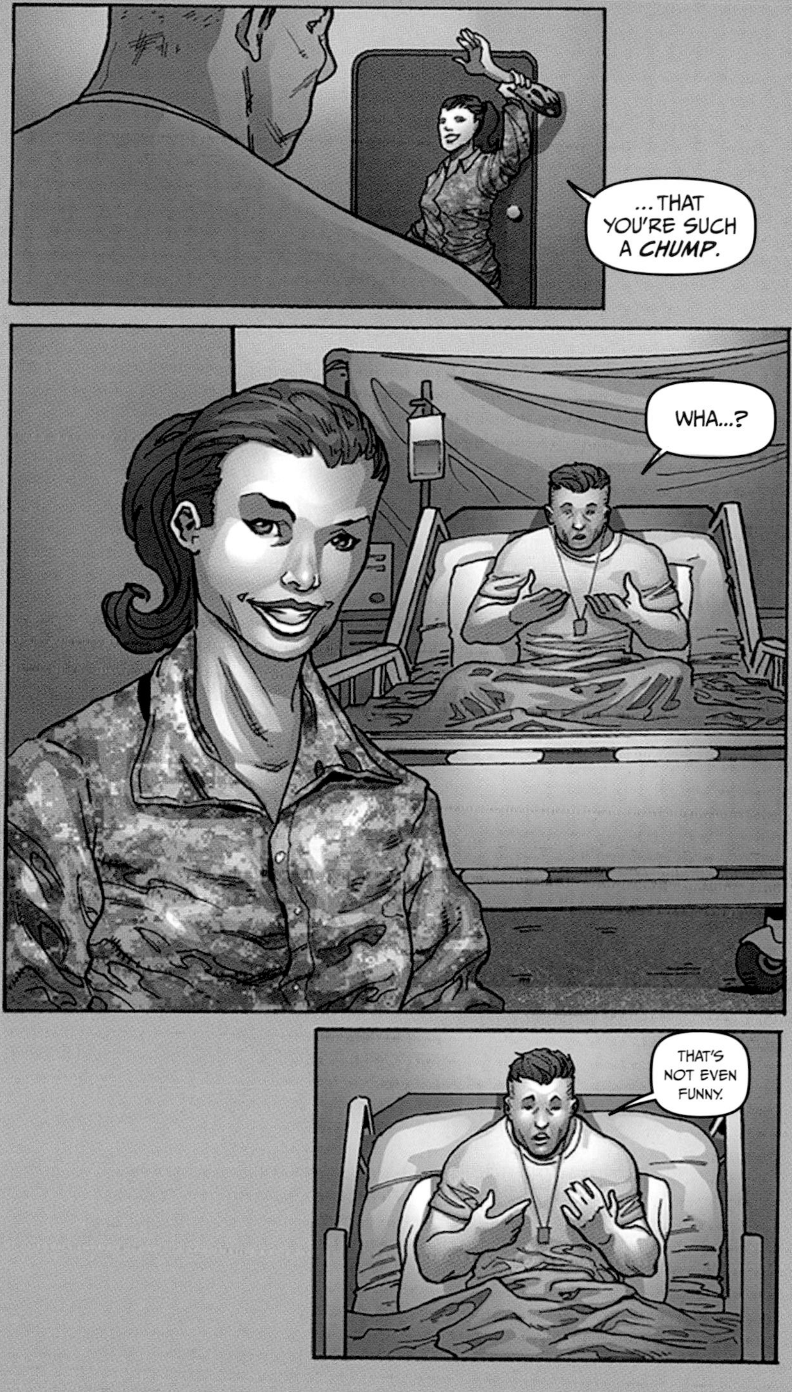
...THAT YOU'RE SUCH A *CHUMP*.
WHA...?
THAT'S NOT EVEN FUNNY.

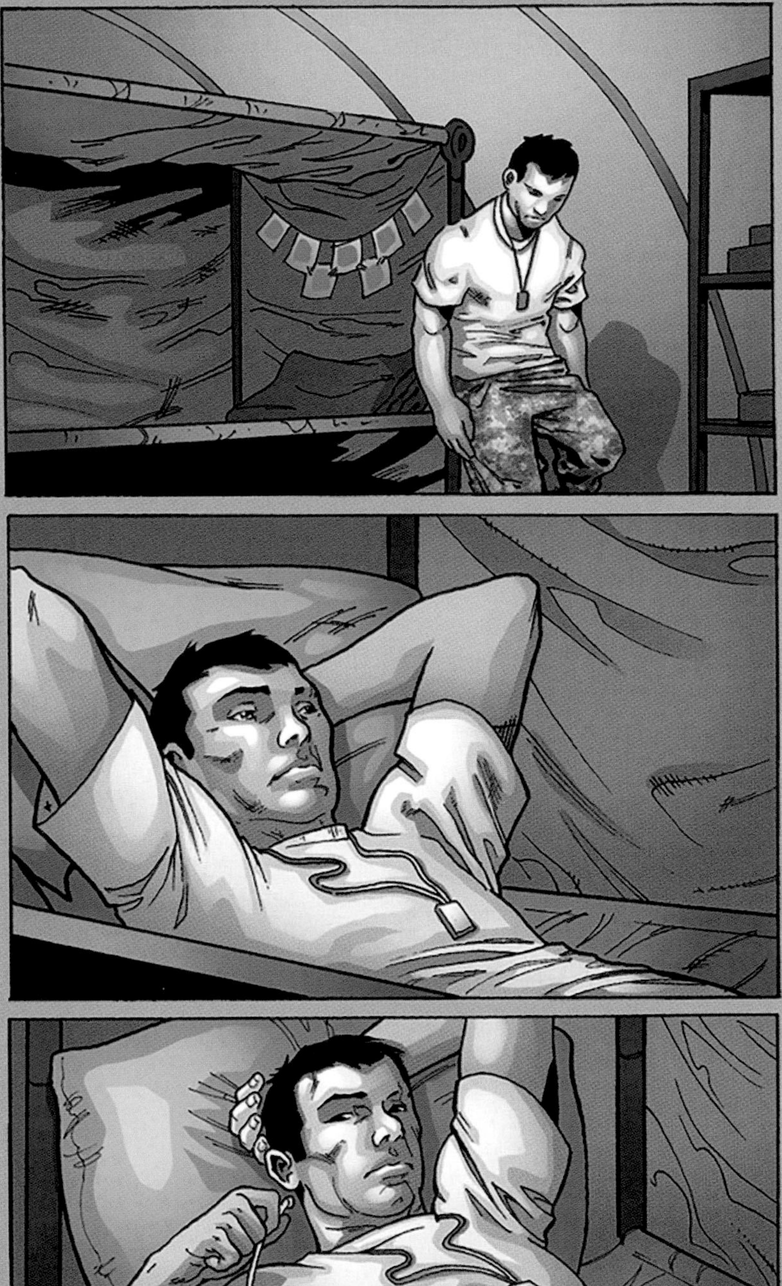

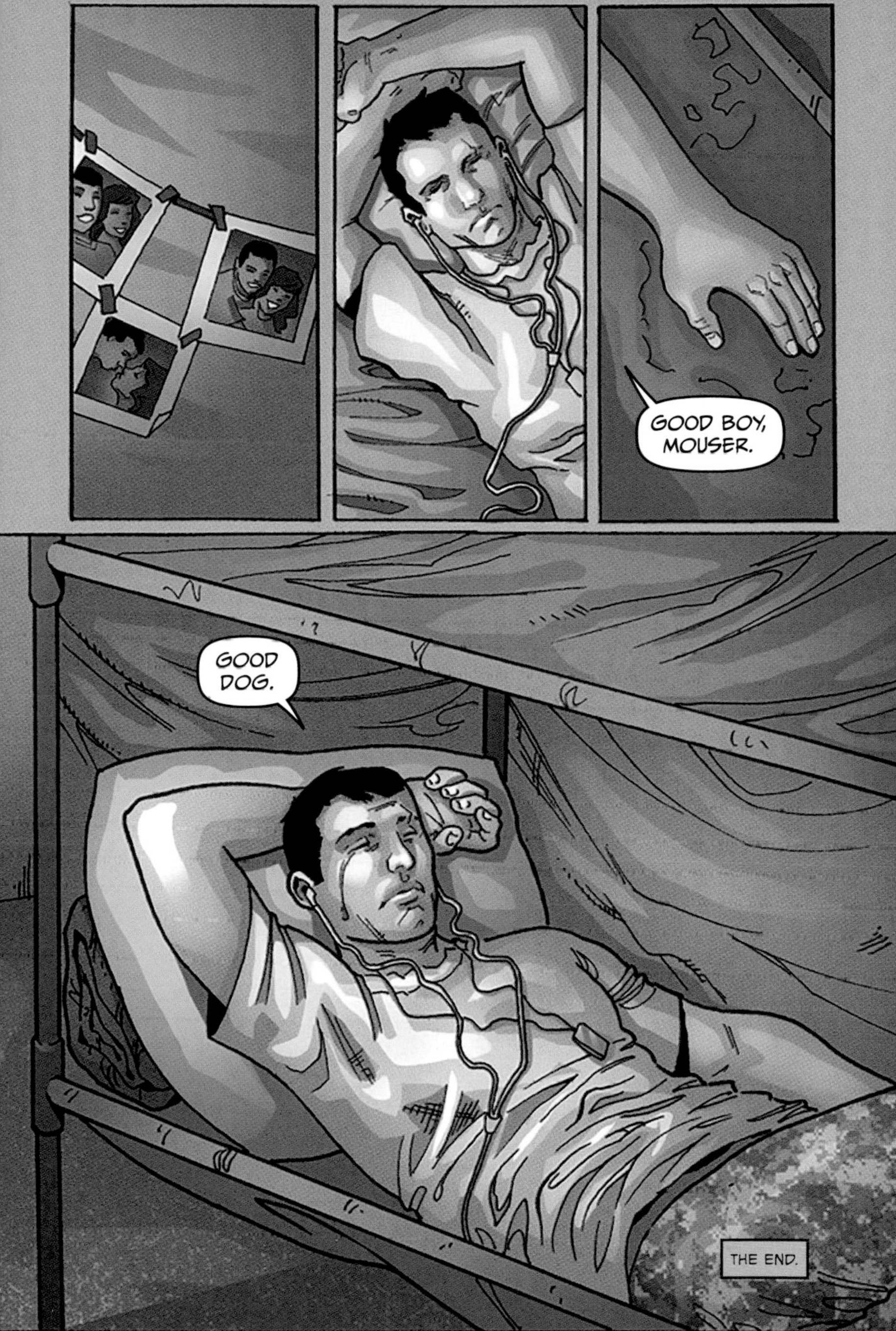
GOOD BOY, MOUSER.
GOOD DOG.
THE END.

EOD
SOLDIERS

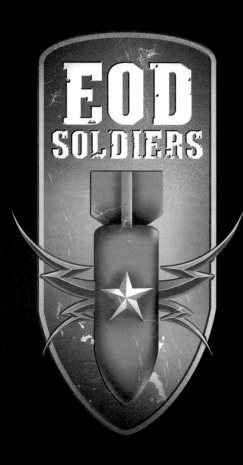

★EOD MEMORIAL★

On February 14, 1969, the Explosive Ordnance Disposal (EOD) Memorial committee formed. The men and women on the committee met with the intent to create a memorial to honor the bravery and sacrifice of fallen EOD soldiers. They chose the Naval Ordnance Station in Indian Head, Maryland, as the original site of the memorial. About one year later, the memorial came to life in the form of four white stone slabs, called cenotaphs. Each cenotaph represents one of the four branches of the military. A bronze tablet was placed on every cenotaph.

During the 1970 dedication ceremony, the first 69 names were engraved on the bronze tablets. These names were U.S. military service members who died on active duty as a result of an EOD mission since the start of World War II (1939–1945). Today, more than 300 EOD servicemen and women from the Navy, Army, Air Force, and Marines are honored on the memorial.

In 1999 the EOD school moved to Eglin Air Force Base in Eglin, Florida, and the memorial moved with it. The new memorial followed the old design with four white cenotaphs and bronze tablets. It's located across from the main EOD school building.

A memorial ceremony takes place on the first Saturday in May of every year. At this ceremony members of the EOD community, as well as their friends and family, gather to remember fallen EOD soldiers. Also during the ceremony, new names are added to the bronze tablets.

Throughout the rest of the year, the memorial is open to visitors seven days a week, except on Thanksgiving and Christmas. A complete list of fallen EOD soldiers can be found on the EOD Warrior Foundation's official website.

VISUAL QUESTIONS

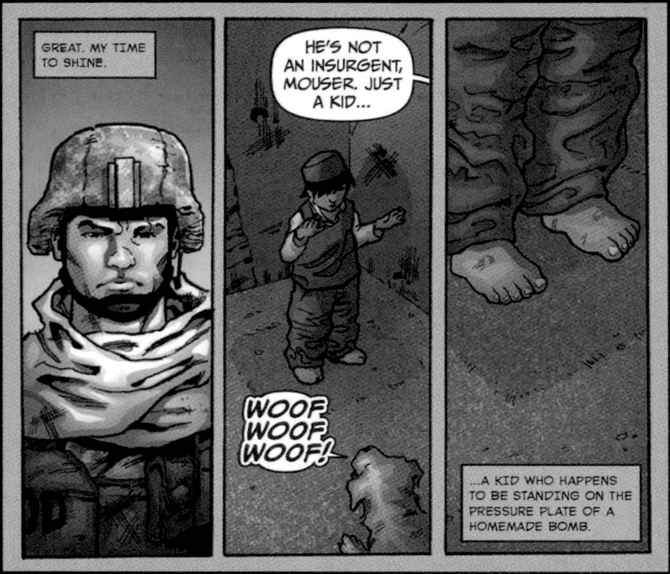
GREAT. MY TIME TO SHINE.
HE'S NOT AN INSURGENT, MOUSER. JUST A KID...
WOOF WOOF WOOF!
...A KID WHO HAPPENS TO BE STANDING ON THE PRESSURE PLATE OF A HOMEMADE BOMB.

1. Why does the author use three panels in this sequence instead of just one? Which panel impacts you the most? Explain why.

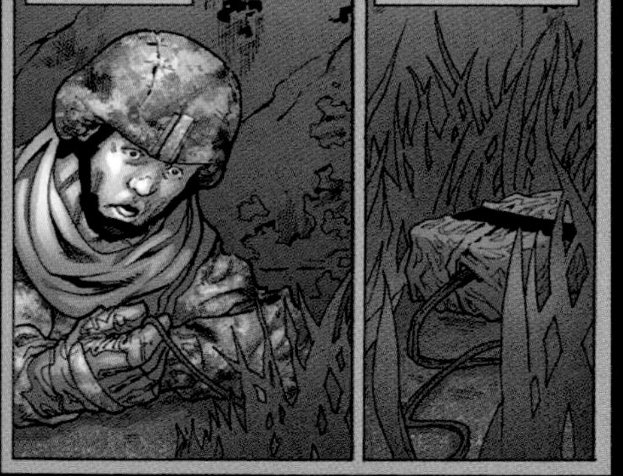
THERE WE GO. DINOSAUR BONE NUMBER TWO.
OH, MAN. THIS IS EASILY 50 PLUS POUNDS OF EXPLOSIVES.

2. How would you describe the look on Dan's face in the first panel? How does the second panel help explain his expression?

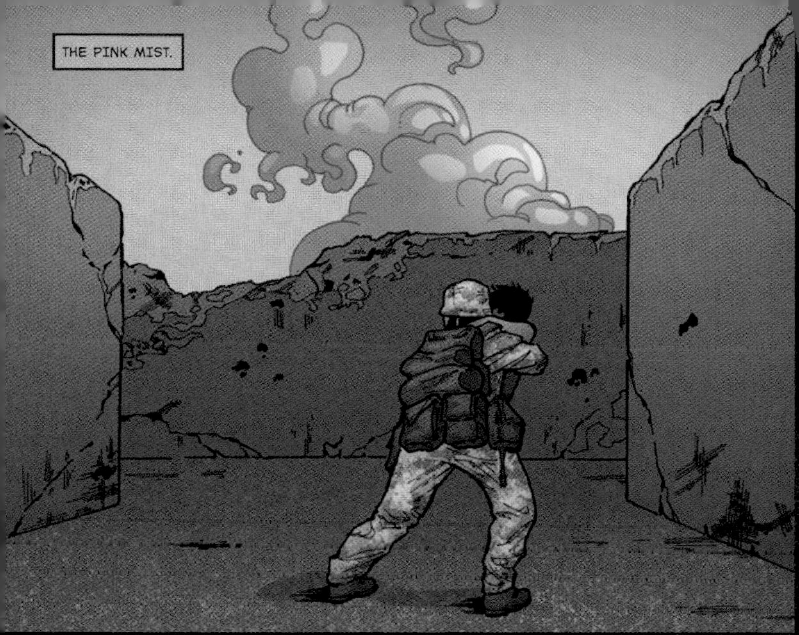
THE PINK MIST.

3. Why is Dan alarmed by the sight of the pink mist rising over the wall? What does he think it means?

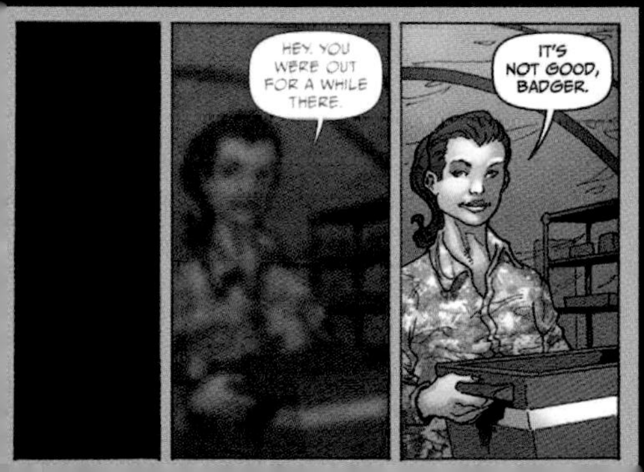
HEY. YOU WERE OUT FOR A WHILE THERE.
IT'S NOT GOOD, BADGER.

4. Why is a black panel followed by a blurry panel in this three-panel sequence? What does it tell us about Badger, the character Campbell is addressing?

AUTHOR

Matthew K. Manning is the author of more than 40 books and dozens of comic books. His work ranges from the Amazon top-selling hardcover, *Batman: A Visual History*, to the children's book, *Superman: An Origin Story*, to a series of graphic novels featuring the military's bomb squad in Afghanistan. Over the course of his career, he has written books starring Batman, Superman, Spider-Man, Wolverine, the Joker, Scooby-Doo, Iron Man, Wonder Woman, Flash, Thor, Green Lantern, Captain America, the Hulk, Harley Quinn, and the Avengers. Currently one of the regular writers for IDW's comic series, *Teenage Mutant Ninja Turtles: Amazing Adventures*, Manning has also written for several other comic book titles, including serving as one of the regular writers for *Beware the Batman, The Batman Strikes!, Legion of Super-Heroes in the 31st Century,* and *Teenage Mutant Ninja Turtles: New Animated Adventures*. He lives in Asheville, North Carolina, with his wife, Dorothy, and his two daughters, Lillian and Gwendolyn.

GLOSSARY

compound (KAHM-paund)—a group of buildings often enclosed by a fence or a wall

detonate (DE-tuh-nayt)—to explode or to cause something to explode

distraction (dis-TRAKT-shunn)—something that draws attention away from something else

fossil (FAH-suhl)—the remains of plants or animals that are preserved in rock

IED (EYE-ee-dee)—stands for improvised explosive device; a homemade bomb often made with material not usually found in bombs

insurgent (in-SUR-juhnt)—a person who rebels and fights against his or her country's ruling government and those who support it

LT (EL-tee)—stands for lieutenant; a rank in the U.S. military above sergeant and below captain

medic (MED-ik)—a soldier trained to give medical help in an emergency or during a battle

paleontologist (pale-ee-uhn-TOL-uh-jihst)—a scientist who studies fossils

trek (TREK)—a slow, difficult journey

MORE EOD SOLDIERS

EOD SOLDIERS
TWO SIDES
MANNING
FURUZONO
LIMA

EOD SOLDIERS
THE MIST
MANNING
FURUZONO
LIMA

EOD SOLDIERS
THE LIST
MANNING
FURUZONO
LIMA

EOD SOLDIERS
GO SLOW
MANNING
FURUZONO
LIMA

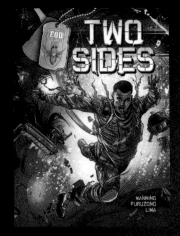

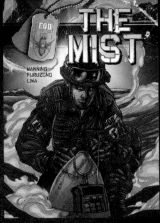

Find cool websites and more books
like this one at www.facthound.com

Just type in the Book ID:
9781496531087
and you are ready to go!